LUCY AND THE DUKE OF SECRETS

SOFI LAPORTE

http://www.sofilaporte.com

sofi@sofilaporte.com

c/o Block Services
Stuttgarter Str. 106
70736 Fellbach, Germany

Editor: Tiffany Shand
Cover Art: Covers and Cupcakes

ISBN: 978-3-9505190-1-3

❀ Created with Vellum

To Cesar, with Love

CHAPTER 1

"*E*xcuse me, sir. I need your help. I missed the stagecoach." Lucy clutched her travel-worn carpetbag as she addressed the burly man behind the bar. He turned to her with a frown.

She held her breath as his sharp, beady eyes appraised her figure, noting her drab brown dress, her threadbare pelisse. She tugged at the bonnet ribbon, setting it askew, so her unruly, bouncing curls spilled over her eyes. She flipped her hair away. Darting a glance at his face, she saw the disapproving set of his jaw. He'd see a girl travelling alone, without a companion. Without any class, style, or money.

"Not my problem." He turned away to pick up a dirty rag. With his other hand, he picked up a wine glass, and proceeded to polish it with a squeak.

"Please. I need to be at Ashmore Hall before nightfall." Lucy twisted her hands in an agitated manner. She felt the first flutters of panic unfurl in her stomach.

He paused. "Ashmore Hall, eh? The Duke of Ashmore's Residence?"

"The very same."

A look of alertness entered his eyes. "You in service there?"

Lucy hesitated. "Well…"

"You're starting out, maybe?"

"I'm new there." That was definitely true.

The innkeeper's face softened. "My daughter's in service, too. Up North. The Duke of Ashmore doesn't just employ anyone. Tough luck, starting the first day late. You'll lose your job before you've even begun."

"Can't you help me?" She couldn't afford to stay at the inn. Her breath quickened at the thought of having to spend the night by the side of the road.

He set the glass down. "You sure you want to go there?"

"Oh, yes. It's urgent."

"Very well." He jerked his chin toward the window. Outside, a man loaded bushes onto a cart. "Try talking to that fellow over there. He's on the way to Ashmore Hall. Ask him for a ride."

Lucy could have hugged him. Instead, she quirked a relieved smile at him. "Thank you! I'll not forget your kindness."

THE MAN IN THE OUTER COURTYARD WAS TALL AND ROUGH-looking. He carried a Hawthorne bush over his shoulder, a second under the other arm. The cart was almost full.

"Sir?" Lucy stepped in his path.

"Move aside," he growled. "This is heavy stuff coming through." He stepped around her and dropped the plants onto the cart. Then he pulled out a rope and tied it around the end of the wagon to keep them from falling off.

"Yonder innkeeper informed me you could give me a ride. I missed my coach and the next one arrives tomorrow, late in the afternoon. But I can't wait that long."

The man made no appearance of having heard a word she'd said. He climbed into his seat.

She followed him. "Please?"

"Do I look like I drive a stagecoach?"

But Lucy would not be deterred. "It would be so very kind of you if you'd take me along."

"There's no space."

"Up here next to you there is, if you moved aside a bit? I don't need so much space. It's just me and my bag here." She patted her carpetbag.

The speckled hat shadowed the man's face. "Move, girl, you are making my horses nervous."

"Please, please, please take me along, I really need to reach Ashmore Hall by nightfall. I won't be a bother." The pitch of her voice elevated to a panicked squeak.

He lifted his whip, then froze. "Ashmore Hall?"

"Yes."

The man turned and looked at her for the first time, taking in her travel-worn clothes and dusty boots. She held her breath. "Are you employed there?"

"What if I am? I need to be there before night falls. I can't afford a room here."

He stared at her with hooded eyes. Then he shrugged and let his whip slash through the air.

The cart rumbled slowly towards the gate. She threw her bag down in frustration. It landed in a puddle. "Oh, blast it all. Why can't Arabella live in a more accessible place? Now what am I to do?"

The carriage came to a halt. The man stared ahead, immobile. Then he called out, "What're you waiting for, girl? I haven't got all day."

It took Lucy a moment to comprehend what he meant. Relief swept through her. She picked up her muddied bag and scrambled into the driver's seat next to him.

"Thank you, oh, thank you, thank you," she said, breathlessly. Then she clung to his arm as the carriage set in motion again, and she nearly tumbled out again.

"I've a feeling I'll regret this," he muttered as he untangled himself from her.

AN HOUR LATER, THE MAN SCRUBBED A WEARY HAND OVER HIS face. "Heaven help me. Do you ever stop chattering?"

Lucy beamed at him. "I do like to talk, don't I? So, you're the head gardener at Ashmore Hall? How wonderful! I heard the gardens of Ashmore Hall are like the gardens of Eden."

He grunted.

"Tell me, what're you working on now? Are you planting those bushes? Are you going to plant them in a huge, impressive alley like they usually have in those grand places?" She waved her hands around.

"Ashmore Hall has alleys a plenty. This one'll be a grove," he said, unwillingly.

"Oh! I can just see it! How lovely it'll look! And then you will surely plant lots of hyacinths, daffodils and gooseberries? How lovely it'll smell!"

"That's an odd combination."

"Is it? But you've got to see the colours in your inner mind, see. It's all about the vision." She spread both hands out in front of her, as if framing a painting.

"The vision." He scratched his nose.

"Yes. Like an artist. I've always thought gardeners are like artists. Like painters of nature." She looked at him dreamily. "You've got to have the vision."

"Devil take it, I've no idea what you're talking about."

"It's easy, see? You close your eyes and visualise it with your inner eye. See the colours and then—an artist would try to catch it with his oils, and oh, a musician with music, a gardener, I suppose, with flowers. A gardener is an artist like all the others. He must be, else he cannot catch the spirit of beauty. The beauty of nature."

The man looked at her as if she'd lost her mind entirely. He dug into his pocket to retrieve a pipe. He lit it and stuck it into the corner of his mouth.

"Sit down before you fall off," he commanded.

Lucy had got on her feet, gesturing about. She plopped down again. "But what am I saying? Do you know we haven't even properly introduced ourselves? My name is Lucy Bell." She held out her hand.

The man stilled. "Miss Bell." His eyes narrowed. "Of course you are."

He didn't take her hand, so Lucy dropped hers.

"And you are?"

He muttered an oath.

"Excuse me?" She tilted her head sideways.

"Henry," he said. "My name is Henry."

"Henry? Just Henry? I can't call a stranger by his first name! Though perhaps we're no longer strangers, not after having talked to each other all this time." She paused. "You could say we're almost friends, can't you?"

"Friends! Good lord. It's more of a one-sided jabbering on your side and me not getting a word in." He pulled himself together. "Henry Gardener at your service."

"Oh, what a perfect name! I suppose it's from centuries of your family working at Ashmore Hall. It's like being called Fisher, or Shoemaker, or Miller, I suppose, one's name reflecting one's occupation. But Bell?" She pulled a face. "It doesn't say much. It'd be nice to be called something more elevated. Something medievally Germanic. Like Isolde, or

5

Swanhilda or Kunigunde. My parents didn't even have a mind to name me Lucinda. No. Just plain, unoriginal Lucy. If I ever have a daughter, I'll call her Isolde. It's such a strong, knightly name! Oh, isn't this day today wonderful? The sky is blue and the clouds over there are so pretty, and I'm so happy I could burst."

"It'll rain." Henry Gardener cast a worried eye on the black clouds that gathered on the horizon. Distant thunder rumbled. He flicked the whip, and the horses sped up. "What happened that you missed the stagecoach?"

"The axle broke, and it tipped over on the side of the road. We were lucky that no one was hurt. It was a bit of a grand adventure, if you think about it. Except walking through the remaining forest to the inn, with all the luggage in tow, wasn't much fun at all. And then I missed the coach to Somersbrooke village, because it only passes through once a day. Do you think there are highwaymen here?"

"Highwaymen?" He looked taken aback. "Not likely."

"Because it'd be a great lark if one were to show up. Don't you think? I've never seen an actual highwayman yet."

"Even if there were, what would he take? Fourteen bushes?"

"Maybe he'd kidnap me, instead, and ransom me for a high price." After a pause, she added, "You would, of course, rescue me."

Henry snorted. "Would I? Maybe I'd find my bushes more valuable and make sure they're out of the highwayman's reach."

"You disappoint me, Mr Gardener." Lucy gave him a mock frown. "I see you don't have a single drop of knightly chivalry in your body. If you were Saint George, you'd stand by and worry about the dragon trampling some rose bush while it munches the princess. Rest assured; I'd save you if a highwayman ever were to kidnap you." She waved her fist in front of his nose. "I have a mean fist."

He cocked an amused eyebrow at her. "I doubt this would impress the highwayman, who'd be in possession of a pistol. And why the blazes would a highwayman want to kidnap me?"

"Maybe you're a prince, or a duke in disguise for which he could ask a ton of ransom?"

He seemed momentarily speechless. "Balderdash."

"I know. I talk a lot, don't I? And most of it doesn't make much sense, but that's the way I am, I suppose. My friend Arabella says—" She broke off.

"What does she say, your friend?"

"Nothing."

"You're meaning Lady Arabella of Ashmore Hall?"

"Oh." Lucy felt her eyes grow to saucers. "I suppose you'd know her. How silly of me not to realise. Yes, I mean Lady Arabella of Ashmore Hall."

"So, you're not a servant seeking employment." He furrowed his brows. "You're a gentlewoman. One of sufficient rank to be acquainted with the sister of a duke."

She sighed but didn't demur.

"Arabella—that is, Lady Arabella—and I went to Miss Hilversham's Seminary for Young Ladies in Bath. We grew as close as sisters. But I haven't seen her in a while." She counted off her fingers. "I haven't seen her for three years, since I got exp—I mean, since I left the Seminary. It's almost forever."

"What is a lady doing out riding in a common stagecoach? Why didn't Lady Arabella send a carriage? And where is your chaperone?"

"The truth is…" Lucy fiddled with the tassels of her pelisse and avoided his eyes. "The truth is, I set out with my own carriage and chaperone. But the coachman got sick on the way and my companion left me at—another inn. She preferred to stay behind and—and nurse the coachman. He was sick. So, I took the stagecoach, but it broke down. And then I missed the connection. Like I said."

Silence.

He raised one eyebrow sardonically. When their eyes met, she looked away.

"Really." A muscle twitched in his cheek. "How altruistic of your chaperone to want to nurse the ailing coachman."

"Yes, really." She cleared her throat. "But we were talking about Arabella. I mean, Lady Arabella. How well do you know her? You must see her often since she loves the gardens so."

"I see Lady Arabella now and then."

"And her horrid brother, I suppose." Lucy pulled a face.

Henry's pipe fell out of his mouth. He caught it with one hand. "What's wrong with His Grace of Ashmore?"

"He's the most odious person I've ever been so unfortunate to meet in my entire life." She thought for a moment. "Though, admittedly, I didn't actually meet him. Not literally yet, I mean. Not in person."

Henry snorted. "Then how do you know he's so odious?"

Lucy stared ahead and didn't reply. She wouldn't even know where to begin, the list was so long.

"Hmm?"

She made a jerky movement, as if remembering that she was conversing with him. "From Arabella, of course," she rushed on to say. "I mean, what she tells me. From what Arabella used to read to me from his letters at school. He disapproves of me. I'm a corrupt influence and what not. And then, once—"

"Once…?" Henry prompted.

"Oh, nothing." Lucy shook herself, trying to rid herself of a particularly pernicious memory. Then she laughed. "Well, he's probably right. I can be a terrible person sometimes. My head is full of nonsensical ideas and I say whatever comes to my mind. It's the first time I'm visiting Ashmore Hall. Arabella insisted." She clamped down her hand on his arm. "Oh look! Stop. Stop! You have to stop."

Startled, Henry pulled to a halt. They were on a little stone bridge crossing a little river. In the water floated a ragged parcel that emitted mewling noises.

Lucy didn't think twice. She threw her carpetbag at Henry, jumped off the cart and ran to the edge of the bridge. The parcel drifted underneath. Lucy ran to the other side and strained to reach the parcel as it passed by. Her arms were too short. She picked up a stick that lay by the road to fish it out, to no avail. She teetered forward, flailed, and— Splash, fell head over heels into the brook.

"Bloody hell, now she's gone and drowned herself." Without a second thought, Henry tossed her bag to the side, leapt off the cart and jumped after her. Just in that moment, thunder rolled, and lightning flashed through the sky.

The leaderless and frightened horses bolted.

CHAPTER 2

*L*ucy sat in the brook, her hair plastered to her head and her dress drenched. Her bonnet swam down the brook. She clung to the parcel, which gave forth odd whining noises.

Henry, equally wet, rubbed the water from his eyes. "What the devil, woman!"

"Kittens! It's a parcel full of kittens about to drown! How can people be so cruel?"

"Kittens. Lord, help me. And my cart?"

Both stared after the bolting horses and carriage as they disappeared beyond the horizon.

"Oh, lord, there go my bushes. And it's raining cats and dogs. Literally."

Thunder rumbled and lightning flashed, as if the gates of hell had opened. Henry and Lucy sat in the brook as rain drummed down. Henry struggled up, slipped, and fell in lengthwise and went under with his head. He emerged, spluttering. Lucy bit her lip. The corner of Henry's mouth twitched. Their eyes met.

Then both, as if on command, burst into laughter.

"I thought this river was deeper, and that you needed rescuing," Henry looked at the water, which reached his knees.

Lucy gasped with laughter and held her side. She sat with legs extended and the water reached her chest. In her arms, she held the wriggling bundle. After she caught her breath again, she said: "I thought, too, that the river would be deeper. But even if it had been, I know how to swim so the rescuing part wouldn't have been necessary. Oh dear. Now the cart and horses are gone."

Another crash of lightning.

"And the bu-bu-bushes! Racing down the lonely country road." She broke into another peal of laughter as she envisioned the loaded cart without its driver.

Henry looked up at the pouring sky. "Heaven help me. This can't be happening. Sitting in a brook with a damsel and a kitten, horses and carriage gone, a storm crashing about us."

He held out a hand and pulled Lucy out of the brook. Now it poured even heavier than before. Not that it mattered, because they were already wet from head to heel.

Henry frowned. "This is not good."

Lucy unpacked the mewling package and expected a kitten to come forth. Her surprise was big when, instead, she lifted out a little black-chequered spaniel. It wiggled its tail and licked and bit her fingers.

"Oh, look at this, an adorable puppy! But how can they just throw him into the river like that! How cruel, heartless and entirely evil people can be!"

Henry took the pup from her hands and inspected it. "It has only three legs." Indeed, the little pup had a stump for a fourth leg.

"So? Is that a reason to kill him? Just because he is missing a limb?" Lucy's eyes flashed. "How dare they? The real defects, let me tell you, are of the character. Those who lack a heart and a soul, those who kill and torture innocent creatures. They're the true cripples in this world! I'd rather miss a limb than a heart!" Lucy wagged her finger into Henry's face as if everything were his fault.

He looked at her, his head slightly tilted, a slight smile on his lips. "No doubt you're right, Miss Lucy."

"And if I ever catch that villain who tried to drown this adorable pup, oh I will smack my fist into his face and bundle him up and throw him right into this river myself!" She thrust her fist under Henry's nose.

Henry gave a slight laugh. "I entirely agree. I will gladly help you with that. And it's a she, by the way."

"And—oh. What?" Lucy, who had talked herself into a rage, had a hard time processing that Henry was amused, but in entire agreement.

"The pup. It's a girl." The puppy now barked and playfully bit Henry's fingers. He returned her to Lucy.

Henry slunk his wet hair back with both hands and she could see his face, which was no longer hidden by hair and hat.

"But—you're quite young!" Lucy stared at him. "I thought you were older. Like very much older."

She felt shy. He looked at her, and Lucy realised her wet dress clung to her every curve. Shyly, she held the puppy in front of her as a shield.

"Deuced awkward situation, this." Henry muttered. "We need to get out of the storm and think about what to do. With some luck, the horses ran home."

Lucy took a step, slipped, and fell into the brook again, dragging Henry with her.

He emerged from the river, spluttering.

Lucy couldn't help herself. She burst out laughing.

THEY SPOTTED A FARMER'S HUT IN THE MIDDLE OF THE meadow and trudged towards it. Henry carried her carpetbag, while Lucy carried her puppy bundle.

"This isn't good," she informed Henry over the drumming rain. "It's my only dress." She only had a second petticoat in her bag, along with a scarf, a bundle of letters and a purse with a few coins.

"We'll stay at that farm until the storm has passed. Hopefully, they have dry clothes there. You have the talent to attract all sorts of disasters. First, you miss the coach. Then you spook the horses, so they bolt. And now it's raining. Scratch that. It doesn't rain, it pours." He glared at her.

"Right, well, blame your toothache and the state of the world on me as well while you are at it," she replied with chattering teeth.

"I don't have toothache." He lifted his hands hastily, as if warding off a curse. "But now you mentioned it, no doubt both my wisdom teeth will start throbbing any time." Henry took off his coat and put it around her shoulders. He looked magnificent as the wet shirt clung to his muscles. Lucy looked away and swallowed.

They walked over the meadow towards a farmer's hut. Lucy knocked delicately on the door. "There's no one there."

Henry hammered on the door with his fist. After a while, a buxom woman opened. She gave them a swift look and started to close the door. Henry jammed in his foot.

"We had an accident on the road. We lost horse and cart and need some shelter until the storm passes."

The woman stemmed her hands against her hips and pursed her lips.

"Married?"

"Er—" Henry looked at Lucy.

"Of course," Lucy stuck her nose into the air, all lady. "We married a fortnight ago. We're on the way home to visit his parents. His mother is so ill. When the storm broke, the carriage tilted, and the horses ran off."

Henry cleared his throat. "Just so."

The woman crossed her arms. "I can offer you the shed for the night. It's clean. There's fresh straw in there."

"For my—w-wife a room in the house, while I take the shed," Henry argued.

"The shed's perfect for Bartimaeus and me," Lucy said at the same time.

"Shed only. For all of you. Take it or leave it." The woman narrowed her lips in disapproval.

"Out of the question—"

"We'll take it," Lucy said with determination. "Bartimaeus needs to get dry before he catches a cold."

The woman sniffed. "Go on then. It's behind the house."

"My name is Henry, not Bartimaeus," Henry told her as they trudged to the shed.

She held up the puppy. "Bartimaeus, meet Henry, unlikely knight in shining armour."

"A male name for a female puppy?"

"She needs all the help she can get in this sad world. A strong, male name is the least thing I can give this poor, unfortunate pup," Lucy lectured. "You should remember that when you ever have to name your own children."

"Lord help me," Henry muttered as he pushed the shed's door open.

THE SHED WAS AN OLD, RUSTIC HUT THAT HAD NO OTHER function than to house an occasional horse or other animal. It had a fireplace, a rickety table with two chairs and fresh hay piled in a corner. Bartimaeus sniffed around, made a puddle behind an old footstool, then curled up in one corner and promptly fell asleep.

"Poor little mite." Lucy petted Bartimaeus who flicked her ears in her sleep.

The woman followed them into the hut.

"You can make a fire in the fireplace but don't burn down the entire hut," she instructed them. "There are blankets here. Clothes. They're old but clean." She dropped a bundle of clothes and blankets on the table, together with a tallow candle, and left again.

Lucy felt the dampness of her clothes creep into her bones, and her teeth clattered. She grabbed one of the woollen blankets and wrapped it around herself. She ought to get out of her wet clothes, but that was impossible with Henry in the same room.

"Y-y-you make the f-f-fire."

Henry knelt in front of the fireplace, and in no time a fire blazed. Its warmth spread through the little room quickly, dipping the room in a cosy orange light. Frowning, he stuck the poker into the fireplace to shift a piece of log around.

The woman returned with a tray of food, a jar of warm milk and two mugs. "Milk, bread, apples and cheese. Tomorrow you are gone at dawn."

"God bless you," Lucy told her. The woman nodded and left. "She is grumpy, but she has a good heart," she told Henry, who grunted yet again in agreement. "Are you in a temper?" Lucy tilted her head to one side, noting the thunderous frown on his forehead. "What happened was unfortunate, but you have to see the silver lining in this situation. Look, we have dry blankets, a fire, and food! Besides the very fact we're in the middle of a thrilling adventure. I wonder what it is like to sleep on that hay. Dear me, how it is raining outside. Did you see the lightning flash? Now, if you stand over there in that corner and look out of the window, I can pretend you are not in the room and change into these dry clothes."

Henry snapped out of his moodiness. "I will go over to the house and convince the woman to give you a proper room." Before Lucy could reply, he grabbed his pile of clothes and rushed outside.

Lucy seized the moment to peel off her wet clothes, which were plastered to her skin. She dried herself and slipped into the dress the woman had given her. It was a coarse, brown linen that hung off her slender frame like a sack.

She curtsied. "What do you say, Bartimaeus? Now I look like a proper farmer's wife."

Bartimaeus replied with a gentle snore.

Henry returned with a black scowl on his face. He'd changed out of his wet clothes as well and looked odd in linen shirt and trousers that were too short for him. Lucy grinned.

"They only have one bedroom and her bedridden husband needs the bed. The man looked more dead than alive. It would have been irresponsible to make him give it up."

"Oh, poor man. It really can't be helped, can it? I must say, I rather like this adventure. It's better than being held up by highwaymen." She twirled.

Henry threw her an irritated look. "You appear uncommonly happy to be stranded here."

"I tend to be a happy person, Mr Gardener," Lucy informed him. Then her stomach growled. "Hurry, or else there won't be anything left for you. I don't think I've ever tasted anything so divine as this simple piece of bread and this cheese." She bit with gusto into a slice of bread.

Henry's stomach grumbled. He sat down on a rickety stool across from her and picked up a slice of cheese.

The fire flickered, and a warm cosiness spread throughout the little room. Lucy had never felt as content as this. What an adventure she was having! This was almost better than at the Seminary. Lucy felt a pang. No, nothing was better than the Seminary. But this was getting close. She felt something which she'd only ever felt at Miss Hilversham's: she felt safe. Safe with him.

Lucy peeped at him through her eyelashes. He was tall and muscular. No doubt that came from all the garden work. He radiated solidity, strength, and warmth. Like an oven that one would want to snuggle up against. The man also seemed somewhat morose. He hadn't stopped frowning since the river. Losing his plants and carriage must have hit him hard.

"Before this continues, we need to get one thing clear." He set down the piece of bread he'd been eating.

"Before what continues?" Lucy said in between two bites.

"This entire situation. It's entirely improper. You are a lady. No, don't argue. If they discover we spent the night here —together—what do you think will happen?"

"I don't know. What?"

"You can't be that naïve." He got up and strode up and down the length of the hut. His head nearly touched the roof beam.

"What's to happen?" Lucy shrugged. "We got caught in a storm. We had to seek shelter. End of story."

Henry pulled his hand through the tousled hair that kept falling over his eyes. "They will have found the carriage and horses by now. And someone must miss you because you didn't arrive. With or without a companion. They will enquire and find us. It'll be a deuced scandal. You'll be completely and utterly ruined, and that, my girl, will be for life."

Lucy licked her fingers and cut off another piece of cheese. She wondered whether it was possible to lose a reputation where there was none, and whether it seemed to matter to begin with. She decided it didn't.

"You have nothing to say to that?" He stood in front of her, his hands on his hips.

"Well. That sounds rather worrisome, the way you put it. I'd rather not be ruined for life. So, I suppose what we must do is to be cleverer than the rest and make sure they don't find us together."

Lucy watched, fascinated, how he lifted one of his eyebrows. She found that she liked his eyebrows. They expressed strength. As did his nose and his jaw. His entire face, in fact. Clean, strong, masculine. And his hands were gardener's hands. Rough working hands, strong, reliable hands that would never let one down...

"How do you plan on doing that?"

"Wha—what?" she swallowed, and their eyes met. She looked away quickly.

"Being cleverer than the rest."

"Easy. I get off the cart a mile before we reach Ashmore Hall. No one will know we even met."

"The cart is gone, if I may remind you."

"We'll hire one from the farmer."

"With whose money?"

Lucy wrapped a curl around her finger as she thought. "Lady Arabella's. We'll tell the woman here Lady Arabella will send a pouch with the money as soon as we've reached Ashmore Hall. Don't worry. Arabella won't breathe a word. Neither will the woman here, if we pay her enough."

"You think the bribe will prevent her from talking?"

"Of course it will. Money solves all problems."

"Does it, now? And you think she would do that for you? Lady Arabella, I mean."

Lucy's eyes widened. "Of course she would! As I would for her. We're like sisters, Arabella and I."

"Hm. You trust her very much, don't you?" He clasped his hands behind his back as he stood in front of her.

"With my life. As she would trust me." Lucy took a sip of milk and started coughing as she remembered the last time Arabella had trusted her. It hadn't ended well. Arabella had nearly drowned in a well. Lucy pushed the unpleasant memory away. "Let's find out tomorrow. I suppose that haystack over there is for sleeping." She draped a blanket over the hay.

She heard him sigh as she dropped on the hay and lay on her side, propping her head in her hand.

She looked up at him. "You can either go outside and wait there in the rain until morning, or you can decide it doesn't matter, lie down over there and tell me a story."

He visibly struggled with himself. Then, as if resigning himself to the inevitable, he dropped down, pulled off his water-logged boots and laid back with his arms under his head, staring at the roof beams.

"I am waiting."

"What kind of story does her ladyship want to hear?"

"Tell me about your childhood. Once upon a time there was a little boy called Henry..."

An involuntary laugh escaped him. Then he told her. Growing up with his brother, how they scampered through the countryside. How they used to go fishing together. How they built a treehouse. How they discovered a cave and pretended to be cavemen for an entire summer. It was semi-dark, with only the orange flicker of the fire in the background.

"And your brother now? Where is he now?"

He was silent.

"Oh no. He—died?"

"Yes."

"I'm so sorry." Lucy's voice was thick.

"I am, too."

"What was his name?"

"David."

"I wish I'd had a brother like David. Even if just for a brief time. Even if it were to mean to have to lose him, eventually."

Her little warm hand crept into his and held on tightly. They were silent for a while.

"You don't have any brothers and sisters?" His voice sounded gruff.

Lucy sighed. "No. It was always my biggest wish to have one. An older brother would have been wonderful to have in one's life. So much in my life would have happened differently, maybe."

"Why do you say that?"

"I suppose—I wouldn't have been so lonely. I lost both my parents early. Having had a sibling would have made a difference."

Henry agreed.

"But let's not talk about me. Tell me what you like best about gardening."

"I enjoy making my hands dirty." He lifted his free hand, inspecting the dirt under his fingernails. "I enjoy digging deep into the earth and feeling mud between my fingers. It's like taking part in creation. Planting a seed and seeing it blossom into a flower. I like the peace of it. Plants are better companions than humans sometimes."

"That sounds bitter." She didn't let go of his hand. "You must love Ashmore Hall very much."

"Certainly."

"That didn't sound too enthusiastic. Let me put this differently. You must love living this life of yours, surrounded by nature every day. Surrounded by—freedom. Yes. Freedom." He barked a laugh. "Oh no, I definitely sense bitterness in that laugh. Pray explain, Henry Gardener. And I want the truth."

"The truth, Lucy Bell? The truth is that I'm a slave to these grounds. My entire life has been predetermined by others. I've been forced to follow in my father's footsteps. My grandfather, my great-grandfather. I've had no choice in my occupation. Of all the choices, possibilities that life offers, always this one thing. Freedom? What freedom?"

"But you said you liked gardening."

"I do. It is a blessing that I do."

"If you'd had the choice, what would you have chosen?"

"I would have been a sailor, maybe. Travel across the seven seas and explore the world."

"Oh yes, that would be quite the adventure. But instead of the land, you'd be tied to the sea? You'd be a slave there, too."

"Maybe, but I would have chosen my fate. True freedom is one of choice. You are a lady. You know nothing of a life tied to the land. Of the toil and strife it entails. The sacrifice it requires. I see you disagree. Why do you shake your head?"

"Because, despite all that, you are so much freer to begin with than women. You may not have been allowed to choose your profession, but in all other ways you are allowed to be free. Women only have two choices: to get married or to become spinsters. Or governesses, which is the same as becoming a spinster." Her face darkened.

Henry propped himself up sideways to search her face in the semi-dark. "How did you end up at the Seminary?"

A variety of emotions flitted over her face. She picked out a piece of straw and folded it into smaller and smaller parts.

"Mother died at birth. Father—died as well." She choked, then talked on quickly, avoiding his eyes. "I was only eight. I got packed up and sent to my great-aunt Jemima. She had money, at least. She said she was too old to care for me, so she arranged I be sent to Miss Hilversham's Seminary."

"And you loved it there."

"It was the best thing that ever happened to me. I met Arabella there. We shared a room. And Birdie and Pen were there, too." Lucy smiled as she remembered her friends. Then her face shadowed again. "Until I had to leave again." Henry waited for her to continue, but she shook her head.

"It is strange, but I have the feeling we have known each other long before we've even met. I feel so comfortable with you, like I never do with anyone else. Do you think that is possible, that souls know each other before they meet?"

"It appears so." His voice was warm.

"Tell me more about what you've planted lately." Lucy felt exhaustion creep into her bones. Her voice was thick with sleep.

And he did. After a while, she began to snore softly. She still held his hand.

He stared thoughtfully into the darkness.

CHAPTER 3

*T*he next day they left before dawn. It was as Lucy predicted. The farmer had a cart that his wife was willing to lend them for the promise of a sum from Lady Arabella. The horse was old, the cart rickety, and their pace was slower than a snail's, but it was a means of transportation.

The day was blustery but cheerful. There was no sign of the previous night's storm. Lucy chattered away. He lit his pipe.

"I would love to smoke a pipe," Lucy burst forth. "It is terribly vulgar, and ladies aren't ever allowed to be vulgar."

He handed her his pipe.

Lucy took a drag and started coughing . "It's—cough—really—cough—quite—cough—good!" She returned the pipe with a grimace.

Henry's lips quirked upward.

"Oh, you have the nicest smile! You look disagreeable most of the time, do you know? It's rather off-putting and makes one wonder what might've happened for you to perpetually look like that. Then you smile! Your eyes lighten up in a million colours of blue and the corners crinkle up in a lovely way. And that sounded like an awkward, badly written love poem, so forget I ever said this. My infernal mouth!"

"Lucy—"

Lucy interrupted him to cover her embarrassment. "I've been lying to you."

He took the pipe out of his mouth. "My eyes don't look like a million colours of blue after all?" he teased.

Lucy blushed. "No, not that."

"You are not friends with Lady Arabella. You have never even met her."

"Of course Arabella and I are best friends. I love her dearly."

"What have you been lying about then? Come tell me, I'm agog with curiosity."

Lucy traced the wooden pattern of the seat with her index finger. "My coachman never got sick and my companion never stayed with him. I don't even own a carriage."

He quirked up a corner of his mouth. "If it makes you feel better, I've figured out that much."

"I did miss the stagecoach. But—" She bit her lip.

"But? Is there more?"

"Arabella doesn't know I'm coming. We haven't communicated in three years. There. Now you know. I'm a terrible person." She hugged her arms to her.

Henry seemed unimpressed. "That certainly is a long string of hideous lies."

She took a big breath. "And there is also something else."

"More?"

Lucy wrestled with herself, then blurted out: "I'm not at all respectable."

She stared into the distance, so she didn't see his brows shoot up.

"I don't follow."

"I'm not—I mean—This is difficult to talk about." She sighed. Henry kept puffing away on his pipe, waiting for her to talk. "I'm a failed governess,"

"That is unfortunate, but I don't see how that would make you not respectable."

Lucy looked down and away.

"So now?" he prompted.

"Now I'm visiting Arabella." She stared blindly at the picturesque meadow that passed by.

"Who doesn't know you are coming? That is awkward. But not necessarily terrible."

She propped her chin on her hand. "Arabella always wanted me to visit her at Ashmore Hall. Except—you know. Her brother."

"Ah, yes. The odious brother. Forgotten all about him."

"He'll throw me out in no time." She swallowed with difficulty.

"Yet you haven't even met the man."

"He's not a man. He's a duke."

"You talk as though he's a god."

"He is. Arrogant and all-powerful, of the worst kind. I'm sorry to be talking like this about your master. Of course, you see things differently and you must be loyal to the family."

"A most unfortunate situation." There was a trace of laughter in his voice.

"Why do I have the feeling you are secretly enjoying my woeful situation?" She frowned. But his face remained dead-pan, his gaze steady.

"Me? I wouldn't dream of it. You have my utmost sympathy."

"There is another reason I am visiting Ashmore Hall." Lucy's forehead knit together. "I need to ask His Grace something of the utmost importance. I need him to write a letter of recommendation."

"Why?"

"So I can return to Miss Hilversham's Seminary. Say. Can I try the pipe again?"

"No." He puffed away at the pipe in contentment. "You already tried it and didn't like it."

"That didn't count because I choked on it."

"You'll choke on it again. Why the deuce do you want to return to the Seminary?"

She felt his body heat next to her, the smell of sweat, tobacco, leather and earth. His left hand lay next to hers, not quite touching hers.

"Because…" she stammered, losing her thread.

"Because?"

"It's my home." She told herself not to snuggle up against his shoulder, which she felt a sudden, inexplicable urge to do.

"I don't understand. Why can you return to the Seminary only with the duke's letter?"

"It's a long story."

Henry looked at the sky. "We have time."

"Oh, very well." Lucy told him how she'd suggested to her friends they'd sneak out of the Seminary at midnight to visit a wishing well. Arabella had made a wish for all of them, upsetting Pen, who insisted on retrieving her coin. Pen had fallen into the well, dragging Arabella down with her. It'd been an accident. Lucy still broke out in a sweat at the thought of how close her friends had come to drowning. "His Odiousness descended in wrathful righteousness and took Arabella out. And Miss Hilversham sent me away. To save the school's reputation." For the Duke of Ashmore had insisted it was all Lucy's fault.

Lucy shuddered as she remembered crouching under the open window, overhearing the ice-cold, arrogant voice slashing her character to pieces. He'd enunciated his words with a damnation that was as clear and strong as if he'd been standing with her in the same room. *Lucy Bell is wild, unpredictable and irresponsible. She is a disgrace to the Seminary...*

It'd been three years ago, but it still stung. She'd felt every bit as worthless as he'd made her out to be. Deep down in her heart she feared maybe, just maybe ... he was right.

"It doesn't seem fair I bear the brunt of the blame when it's been Arabella's fault. It was her idea to throw in those coins." She stared darkly ahead.

He leaned sideways on his knee as he listened. "May I ask what kind of wish Arabella made that had Miss Pen so keen on retrieving those coins?"

"It was rather silly. Arabella wished we'd each end up marrying and living happily ever after with a duke." She uttered the last word with utmost contempt. Henry choked on his pipe. "Not all of us with the same one, silly." Lucy's lips curled.

He coughed a bit more.

"I can't blame Pen for getting so upset about it, though maybe she overreacted a bit. I don't believe in wishing wells. Not that it matters, because I won't ever marry a duke, even if he got down on his knees and begged me."

Henry cleared his throat. "That would be a dreadful fate, indeed. But back to the point. You're thinking, if you can get His Grace to write you a letter—"

"And reinstate his patronship—"

"—then everything will be well again, and you can go back to the school."

"That's the plan."

"And if it doesn't work? If he refuses to write it?"

Lucy swallowed hard, lifted her chin and boldly met his

gaze. "He simply has to! I will make him!"

"You will make him?" Henry's eyes lit up with amusement. "To my knowledge, no one can make His Grace do anything he doesn't want to do."

"I'll think of something." Lucy said grimly. "I'm good at ideas. Maybe a trade of some sort."

"A trade?" Henry grinned.

"Yes. Something he desperately needs."

"That's bound to be a challenge. The man has everything." He crossed his arms and leaned back, thoroughly entertained.

"Everyone always needs something. Including a duke."

She sat some minutes pondering in silence. Then she snapped her fingers. "Ah. I have it!"

"Pray tell."

"Arabella."

"I don't follow."

"I can help him marry off Arabella to someone suitable. Men have no idea about these things." She folded her hands in her lap.

"Dear me," he said.

She drew her eyebrows together. "It's not entirely ethical, is it? To manipulate a dear friend into an arranged marriage, when she's sworn to marry only for love—in return for a stupid letter. How horrible of me to even think of this. I'm worse than Judas."

Henry knocked his pipe against his seat and brushed the ashes away. "This won't do at all. Maybe you should just talk to His Grace and be agreeably surprised that he'll write said letter without any kind of trade, unethical or otherwise."

Lucy shook her head that her curls flew. "You are too positive-minded, Henry. I like that about you."

Their eyes met. His shone bright blue in his tanned face.

Lucy blushed and looked away.

She pointed to the distance. Ashmore Hall appeared in front of them, a sprawling, Palladian structure crowning a hill, a tremendous lake in front, surrounded by Henry's beautiful gardens. "Just look at this—terrible glory!"

"Why terrible?"

"Because it looks terribly intimidating." Lucy gazed at it in despair.

Henry stopped the cart. "It is quite something to look at."

Lucy slumped in her seat. "I'm not doing Arabella a favour by visiting her. It isn't good for her to be seen in my company. They'll say I'm a bad influence. They'll say I'll corrupt her. Yesterday, you said the worst thing that could happen to me is that my entire life becomes utterly ruined from being with you here. Well, it doesn't matter in the slightest to someone who is already considered being on the very bottom of the social scale. So there."

"You are being very hard on yourself, my girl," Henry tugged on one of her curls. His finger brushed her cheek, and Lucy wanted to turn her head and bury her face in his big, warm hand.

"I don't care for all the lofty lords and dandies that parade about there. I would like to marry a normal man. One who is kind and who likes me just for myself. Someone with a little house and a garden. A—a gardener would do nicely. I'm sure I would love to be married to a gardener! It sounds heavenly. I could help with the work and I'm certain I can bake great crumpets, you know? I mean, I haven't actually baked crumpets before, but it can't be that difficult. I'm sure they would turn out fantastic. And in the morning, I can help with the roses, and maybe there would be chickens that need to be fed ... " Her voice petered away. Her face flushed. She'd as good as propositioned marriage to him. And he wasn't responding. He wasn't even looking at her. His eyes were fixed on Ashmore Hall.

"Despite everything, you are a lady and belong to the Hall, Miss Lucy Bell. Your world is not mine." He smiled sadly.

"I know." She choked.

"It's really better to just walk in there, and play along with all the parties, dances, teas and whatever it is you fine folk do, and pick up a dandy and marry him. It is the better life."

"I would so much rather marry a gardener."

As his eyes melted into hers, she saw something in them that tugged at her heartstrings. Lucy felt she could drown in them. His face was close, oh so close. She could count the fine hairs of his eyelashes.

Her heart thudded.

Lucy didn't think. She reached up, pulled his face down towards her, and planted a kiss on his lips. They felt soft, warm, spicy. A feeling like warm honey oozed through her body, leaving a delicious tingling sensation that made her toes curl.

Shocked by her own action, she let go.

"I just kissed you," she blurted out.

"So you did." He blinked.

Her fingers wandered to her lips. "I've never kissed anyone before." She looked at him with enormous eyes. "I don't regret it. Not for a moment."

He reached out and brushed his rough thumb gently over her lips. She quivered. He looked at her for a while longer, a quiet smile lurking in the depths of his eyes.

Something in her lap yipped and bit her thumb. Little Bartimaeus had woken up.

Lucy laughed breathlessly. The spell was broken.

Henry dropped his hands and picked up the reins. "Let us proceed to Ashmore Hall."

Lucy marvelled how it was possible that with a single kiss, her entire world had shifted.

He helped her climb down from the cart about a mile before Ashmore Hall.

"I think you better keep Bartimaeus. She'll be happier romping around with you in the park." She placed the panting bundle into Henry's arms.

"Will I see you again?" She wrapped her arms around herself and fought the sadness welling up.

"I work in the gardens. And you?"

"I walk in the gardens."

"So maybe then, our paths will cross."

"Maybe they will cross. And when they do, you will not know me anymore."

Henry looked off into the distance. "Probably not. I will be too busy with my roses. Nor will you know me."

"Probably not. I will be too busy with the dandies."

"Off with you, then." He swung his reins, and the horses trotted off before she could say more.

She would have had so much more to say.

Then again, maybe it was best he left before she had the chance to blurt out she'd fallen head over heels in love with him.

CHAPTER 4

*D*ukes were ghastly creatures.

Lucy stared across the sweeping lawn at the stately hall that proclaimed century-old dukely grandeur. This ostentatious looking hall was built to impress, impose, and intimidate. Just like their owner.

She felt her stomach knot up into a stone-tight ball. She wanted nothing more than to pick up her skirts and run the other direction, screaming. Back to Henry, and ask him to— well what? He'd already as good as said they had no future together. They were from different worlds. Lucy blinked the tears away and swallowed the hard lump in her throat.

There was no time to be sad. She had something of tremendous importance to accomplish here.

Lucy chewed on her lip as she thought over her plan. It was painful, contradictory, and it went against every fibre in her nature. But it was the only way.

She needed to impress Arabella's brother, the awful Duke of Ashmore. She needed to get him to be the patron of Miss Hilversham's school again.

Lucy would make such a good impression on him that

he'd forget everything that happened in the past, and when she finally asked him to write a flourishing letter of recommendation regarding her very excellent character, he'd retract his hastily spoken words in Miss Hilversham's office, in addition to reinstating his patronship of the institution, even doubling the amount. Then Miss Hilversham would take her back with open arms and she'd be able to return to the Seminary. Her old home.

And everything would be well again.

Lucy slumped.

That was as likely to happen as a unicorn with fairy wings emerging from the forest on her right, but, if her name was Lucy Bell, she'd make it happen.

She plopped down into the grass and pulled out a blade.

Lucy hadn't always hated the Duke of Ashmore. In fact, she never admitted it to herself, but she'd been secretly jealous of Arabella that she had such an important big brother who looked out for her. Who scrawled lengthy, weekly letters and sent packages stuffed with black currant jelly, millefruit biscuits, cardamom comfits, leather-bound books and silken hair ribbons, which Arabella had distributed amongst her friends. Lucy couldn't imagine him picking the black currant jellies; surely that must have been the housekeeper. And the hair ribbons? Would a man as important as the duke go into a haberdashery to choose ribbons for his sister? Lucy doubted it, but a part of her was charmed at the possibility of the idea.

If Lucy were honest with herself, she'd heroised Arabella's brother a tiny bit. Very well, quite a bit. She didn't dare to admit it, but she'd secretly hoped that some of that bountiful brotherly warmth spilled over on her. Just a tiny drop. Surely he'd look benignly upon Arabella's bosom friend? Well, that hadn't happened. Because of him, she'd lost the only home she'd ever known. She'd never forgive him for that.

And now she had to charm him. Get him to open his purse for the school again. With her scatterbrained social graces, infernal chattermouth, and their mutual dislike of each other, that was not likely to happen. Lucy dug her fingernails into the earth.

She had to convince him, somehow. The alternative was too grim to even think about. Where could she go, if not back to Miss Hilversham?

Lucy got up and wandered across the sweeping parkland towards the massive mansion. Her steps faltered, and she gazed up at Arabella's imposing home. She stepped into its shadow and shivered.

When she reached the pebbled drive leading up to a massive staircase in front of the colossal entryway, she was rudely confronted with reality. She could hardly knock on the main door, dressed as she was. She looked doubtfully down her rough linen dress and shawl. Would the toplofty butler even admit her? No. She'd have to find another way inside. Lucy looked for the servant's entrance, which was located in the wing around the corner. Finding the door locked, she pulled the bell, and waited.

A harassed-looking housemaid opened the door. She skimmed Lucy from top to bottom. "Finally. We thought you'd never come. Mind your words, now, for Mrs Bates's been in a temper the entire day."

Before Lucy could put in a word, she was ushered into a dark-looking corridor that smelled of shoe polish, beeswax and lamp oil.

"Wait here."

The girl left.

Lucy didn't think twice. As soon as the girl was out of sight, she hastened down the corridor, opening a door that she hoped would lead to the main rooms. It was the still room.

Lucy closed the door again, turned, and ran smack into a severe-looking woman dressed in funereal black, who, no doubt, was the housekeeper, Mrs Bates.

"And who do you think you are?" She inspected Lucy with a wrinkled nose. Before Lucy could answer "I am Miss Lucy Bell, a guest of Lady Arabella," the housekeeper ranted on.

"Do you know you are late? What impertinence! We've waited for you an entire day! I'd send you back if we were not desperate for more help."

"But—"

"Hush! No excuse can make up for your tardiness. Off to the linen room and fetch yourself a clean apron and cap. Your dress is a disgrace. Show me your hands."

Lucy stretched out her hands. Mrs Bates inspected them through her spectacles, then slapped them. "For shame! There is earth under the fingernails. And the length! Meg!"

The housemaid who'd opened the door, appeared. "Yes, Mrs Bates."

"Take her to the slop room. Have her scrub her hands and pare her fingernails. Make sure she rubs lemon in them. Give her a new dress, take one of the hand-me-downs that we keep for the parish on the shelf in the laundry room. Fetch a clean apron and a cap. Off you go."

Meg took Lucy's elbow. "Come with me."

Lucy was shown the scullery where she scrubbed her nails over the sink. It was curiosity, humour, and a perverted delight for mischief that prevented her from revealing her true identity. They thought she was a servant? Well, then. A servant she would be! She pulled on a faded, but clean pale blue dress and put on the scratchy cap over her curls and tied a starchy apron around her waist.

"Arabella, here I come. Your very own housemaid." She curtsied.

"Annie! To the front parlour! And bring the brushes!" Mrs Bates' sharp voice rang out.

"She means you." Meg popped her head into the room. "You better hurry."

It looked like she was given a new name. And what brushes did Mrs Bates mean? Where could she find them? The black bucket in the corner with—ah yes, they looked like brushes. Lucy picked up the bucket and went out into the hall.

Together with Meg, she dusted and tidied two drawing rooms, the dining room, and the front parlour. She carried coals and linen, cleared, cleaned and polished and lit the grates. Her back hurt and her fingers blistered. She rubbed her aching shoulder. It had been a long day.

Mrs Bates came to inspect their work. She slid a finger over the fireplace mantle to inspect it for dust. Since Lucy had just scrubbed the marble with quicklime and soap until her fingers cracked, she found nothing to complain.

"We finished the rooms up here, ma'am," Meg told her.

"Good. Then start airing the red dining room and help with the napkins. Fast, fast." Mrs Bates clapped her hands. "We're running out of time. They're returning within the hour."

Lucy repressed a groan. Meg pulled Lucy to another room, where another set of activities waited for them.

Meg talked almost as much as Lucy. After only an hour, she knew all the servants' names, ages, who they were, where they came from, along with some personal gossip. Meg also told that she had a sweetheart she hoped to marry but couldn't, because she was tied down in service and needed to save money. That she was afraid of the duke, but even more so of his grandmother. That Lady Arabella was expected to get engaged soon and that they expected the duke's own engagement announcement any day as well.

Arabella, engaged? This was news to Lucy.

"A party of nearly twenty people. They're to stay here for at least a fortnight," Meg groaned. "It's going to be a double engagement, and that's so much work. With so many people in the house, it's difficult to stay out of their way. 'Tis hard. Once, I almost ran into the duke. He never noticed me, but I was terrified. Lady Augusta, the Dowager Duchess, is so odd. She insists I come when she rings the bell in the drawing room to do things that only footmen should do. Me! A mere housemaid! When we've got so many footmen about. I'm scared to make a mistake."

Lucy sympathised. "You forget they're just people too, Meg. Even the duke. Even the dowager."

Meg shook her head. "No, they're not. She ain't no normal person, neither is the duke. They're like gods they are."

Funny, because a few hours ago Lucy had said the same thing to someone else. A hollow pain gnawed in her heart. Henry.

"Do you know a gardener named Henry?" she asked as she stacked the napkins.

"Henry? Never heard of him."

"He's head gardener? He is even called Gardener?"

"Sorry, Annie. Haven't been out much in the gardens. Don't have time." She set down the last folded napkin. "Right. We get to have tea now."

Lucy followed Meg down into the servants' hall, where she was given a cup of strong tea and a piece of shortbread.

So that was a servant's life. Toil, toil, and more toil.

"Lady Arabella just arrived." A footman rushed into the servant's hall, setting it off in a frenzy of activity.

Goodness! Lucy wondered whether Arabella even had an inkling of what impact her arrival had on the servants.

"John, quick, take the tea tray to the blue salon. Her Grace and Lady Arabella are waiting there," the housekeeper told a footman, who was still in the process of drinking his tea. He looked at his teacup regretfully, got up, and scrambled into his scarlet-gold livery coat. It would take a while until he'd buttoned up his waistcoat. Mrs Bates turned to issue orders to the maids.

Lucy acted quickly. She grabbed the silver tray and left the room. In the general busyness of the hall, it would take a while until anyone realised that the tea tray was missing.

CHAPTER 5

*D*ear me, it was heavy! Lucy stumbled and nearly dropped the silver tray in the narrow servant's stairway leading up to the second floor. She'd worked with Meg in the blue salon previously, so she knew where to find it.

"Ah. Finally. Tea. What took you so long? Bring it here, girl," a rusty, masculine-sounding voice said, followed by a stomping of a cane on the floor. It belonged to an elderly woman with snow-white hair and an eagle nose. That must be the Dowager Duchess Augusta Ashmore, Arabella's grandmother. She sat on a French chaise longue and looked up haughtily when Lucy entered. Across from her sat a blonde-headed girl, with a finely chiselled nose and high classical forehead that no doubt was a family heritage. Arabella. She looked pretty in a pink muslin dress. She never looked Lucy's way but kept her head bent over her embroidery. "What are you loitering there for, girl? I said bring it here!"

Lucy placed the tray on a side table, glad that she hadn't toppled the heavy pot with the water. Now she understood why Meg was so terrified of meeting a member of the household. The dowager was intimidating. Her icy grey eyes were sharp and her tongue even sharper.

Another stomp of the cane on the floor.

"What do we have here?" The woman bent forward to inspect the tray.

"Meringues, cucumber sandwiches, and almond tarts," Lucy said after she curtsied.

"Bah. Nothing but sweets and bland vegetables."

"You could add pepper to the cucumber sandwiches," Lucy replied. "Although I daresay a pinch of chilli might be better."

"Chilli! Are you trying to poison me?"

"You could also try some paprika. Not as spicy as chilli, I daresay," Lucy insisted.

Lady Augusta appeared stunned at the audacity of the housemaid. "What? Are you trying to lecture me on what spices I might enjoy?"

"Not at all, ma'am. I was just thinking if you don't like sugar and the only other alternative appears to be bland cucumber sandwiches, one might as well add some spices which you no doubt grow in your beautiful garden, tended by a gardener."

Arabella emitted an unladylike shriek, causing the dowager to drop her cane. Lucy picked it up and talked on. "Next to ginger, pepper, chilli and paprika, one might also try oregano or—"

"Lucy!" Lucy found herself hugged, squeezed and whirled around. "Lucy, Lucy, Lucy! It *is* you! I thought I was dreaming of hearing your voice in this room! What are you doing here! Oh my goodness, and look at you in this outfit! Is this one of your tricks again?" Arabella squeezed her again.

"What? How? Tricks? And who is this Lucy you keep

screeching about?" The dowager groped for her quizzing glass.

"Oh, what joy, my Lucy is finally here in Ashmore Hall, and you never even told me you were coming! It's been so long! You naughty girl, I worried myself sick over you. You never replied to any of my letters. I've so much to tell you." She dragged Lucy to the sofa and pulled her down next to her.

Lucy was laughing and crying simultaneously.

The dowager looked at the pair as if she didn't understand the world anymore. "I just want some tea with a small treat that does not contain sugar, and my granddaughter goes off in hysterics over the maid. What's this world coming to?" she complained.

"Grandmama, this is my best friend, Lucy Bell, with whom I went to the Seminary in Bath. We shared rooms. I told you about her!"

Lucy untangled herself from Arabella's embrace and curtsied.

The dowager stared at her through her quizzing glass. "Why the devil are you parading about in servants' garb, Lucy Bell?"

Arabella giggled. "It's one of her pranks—she does this all the time, Grandmama."

The dowager sniffed. "Does she, now? Somehow this fails to impress me."

"You won't believe what we did back in Bath. Once she dressed up as one of our instructresses, complete with grey wig and spectacles, and led an entire class in front of the headmistress, who never noticed until half an hour passed."

"But only because I made a silly but colossal mistake. I placed Balochistan in China when sketching out the map, which was entirely wrong. The headmistress noticed and fired me on the spot. Until she realised who I was."

"And where, pray, would you place Balochistan now?"
The old woman looked unamused at her antics.

"Why, in Persia, of course."

"It says a lot about this headmistress' intelligence if it took her half an hour to uncover your identity, even though she knew the more precise location of Balochistan. That school in Bath can't have been any good. None of this accounts for your unorthodox garb. Explain!"

She told the story of the broken coach, lost luggage and skipped the part of meeting Henry.

"This was not meant to be a schoolgirl's trick at all, Your Grace. I apologise for my appearance. It was a misunderstanding. My travel dress wasn't—let's say, it's not presentable. I daresay Mrs Bates mistook me for a servant, and she assigned me some tasks to do about the house."

"And it never occurred to you to reveal your identity as a guest."

"Er, no. I admit I was rather curious about discovering all about the life of a servant below stairs."

"And? Was it amusing? To clear out chamber pots?" There was a gleam of interest in the matron's slate-grey eyes.

"Thank heaven I didn't have to do that. I cleared out some fireplaces, though. I had no idea they harbour so much soot!"

Arabella looked disconcerted. "Clear out fireplaces! How can that be possible! I am terribly ashamed our housekeeper is incapable of distinguishing servants from guests. To treat my dearest friend so! Mistake her for a servant! Lucy, I'm so sorry. I shall have a word with Ash about this."

"No! Arabella, no one is to get in trouble over this, least of all Mrs Bates. I insist. It's not her fault!"

"Fiddlesticks! Don't go pestering Ashmore, he's got more important things to worry about. The woman's been hired to select our staff with discretion. She's failed at judging people's characters. Be that as may." The dowager rammed her cane into the floor. "I want my tea now!"

"Here, let me pour, Grandmama." Arabella poured water over the tea leaves and let it steep. She gave Lucy a teacup.

The dowager downed it with one gulp. "Bah, the stuff is terrible. Send for a fresh pot."

Arabella rang the bell.

Meg must have waited outside, for she appeared quickly. Her eyes grew to round saucers when she saw the tea tray and Lucy sitting next to Lady Arabella on the chaise longue.

"A pot of fresh water and the housekeeper," the dowager ordered.

"Yes, ma'am." Meg took another shocked look at Lucy before she left the room.

"Her name is Meg," Lucy said in between two sips of her own cup of tea. The older woman was right. The tea was hideous.

"Excuse me?" The dowager turned her cold, haughty eyes towards Lucy.

"They do have names, you know, Your Grace."

Lady Augusta raised her quizzing glass and stared at Lucy, which would have terrified any lesser mortal, but Lucy with no little effort of stoicism pretended nothing was wrong and forced herself to swallow the detestable brew.

"Well!" The dowager was never left speechless.

"Lucy is like that, Grandmama. She tends to speak up for the servants. She used to lecture us back at the Seminary that we're to treat our maidservants well. She is right."

"How extraordinary. Are you a revolutionary, Miss Bell?"

"No." Lucy chuckled. "I just believe servants are regular people like you and me."

"Bah. I see what you are up to, Miss Bell. You're here to subvert the social order and send us all to Hades. It will be amusing to see whether you succeed." The dowager glowered at Lucy, but there was a twinkle of amusement lurking at the back of her eyes.

"Lucy is as much of a revolutionary as I am, Grandmama." Turning to Lucy, Arabella said, "Oh, what fun that you are finally here! We're having a house party. It's quite the thing of the season. Ash has invited all the important families. They're all out now visiting the Abbey, even though the grounds are still soggy from yesterday's storm. I had a headache, so I returned early to have tea with Grandmama." Arabella bent forward and murmured, "Ash expects me to get engaged. I am to accept Lord Finbar's proposal. He's here, too."

"Lord Finbar. I don't think I've heard of him." Lucy frowned.

"The man is an idiot." The dowager didn't mince her words.

Lucy turned to Arabella. "Is he?"

Arabella smiled, but it didn't reach her eyes. "Never mind Grandmama. She thinks most of the human population consists of idiots."

"And so they are."

"Ash says Finbar is of excellent family. He'll be an earl one day. Ash says a union would benefit all of us. Oh, and he is unbelievably handsome! Easily the best-looking man of the party. Ash says he is perfect for me."

"Ash says, Ash says. And you? Do you think he's perfect for you?"

Arabella hesitated a moment too long, which was all the answer Lucy needed. She refrained from saying more because the door opened and Mrs Bates entered with a pot of fresh tea.

"Ah. Finally. Set it here." The dowager pointed her cane at the table. "And have a good look at this girl next to me. She no doubt looks familiar."

Mrs Bates stared at Lucy. "You! Your Grace—"

"Miss Lucy Bell is a guest here and a friend of Lady Arabella. Memorise her face so you don't mistake her again for a servant."

Mrs Bates blanched. "I apologise, ma'am. This is inexcusable. I shall offer my resignation."

"Fiddlesticks! The girl is to blame as much as you since she didn't bother to reveal her identity. You'll stay in this employment and never again judge people by their appearance. You'll organise a room, proper clothes, and a personal maid for Miss Lucy Bell. This other girl will do. What's her name? I was instructed that their kind has names. Sue. Peg."

"Meg," Lucy interjected.

"Peg, Reg, Meg, same thing." The dowager gave a dismissive wave. "This Meg will be her abigail. That's all."

Mrs Bates looked so crushed when she left that Lucy felt sorry for her.

"Now pour me my tea and don't bother me any more."

Lucy poured her a cup of tea. "I really meant that about the cucumber sandwiches and the chilli, ma'am. You ought to try it."

"You are a saucy, meddlesome minx, Lucy Bell," the dowager said gruffly.

"That means she likes you," Arabella whispered to Lucy.

"I heard that."

"You always hear what you are not supposed to, Grandmama."

"Yes, and I don't hear what I don't want to, which is most of the conversation by those fools that are currently residing in this house. It's truly a blessing to be deaf at times."

Arabella gave her a kiss and went ahead to check whether Lucy's room was ready. Lucy wanted to follow her, but the dowager held her back.

"One thing, Lucy Bell. You are an unconventional thing.

You seem to bring anarchy along wherever you go. That is not necessarily bad. I detest conformity because it is boring and you, for all I can say, are anything but boring. Let me tell you one thing, though." She stamped her cane on the floor for emphasis and leaned forward. Her eyes flashed. "I love my granddaughter to pieces. Her happiness is central to my heart. If you corrupt her, I will throw you out on the street without mercy."

Stung, Lucy straightened her shoulders. "Your Grace," she looked into the older woman's iron eyes, "I, too, love Arabella to pieces. Her happiness is central to my heart as well. I would shoot myself rather than 'corrupt' her. Rest assured, I will leave immediately if I should ever be in the danger of hurting my dearest friend."

"I see we shall get along famously, Lucy Bell."

"I hope so, Your Grace."

Arabella stuck her blonde head through the open door. "Are you coming, Lucy? They put you right next to my room, which is fabulous! The party's returning and we need to get ready."

"I don't suppose I should meet them in this outfit." Lucy looked down at her wrinkled and stained housemaid's dress.

"You can have all the dresses you want, Lucy. I've so many I don't know what to do with them."

"Yes, yes, go play dress up. I need a nap." The Dowager Duchess leaned back and closed her eyes.

"Good afternoon, Your Grace." Lucy curtsied and left the room calmly, but inside she was in turmoil from her exchange with the dowager. Corrupt influence, she'd said. Lucy's heart cramped. Why did everyone believe the worst of her? She sighed as she followed Arabella down the corridor.

CHAPTER 6

*L*ucy's room was a generous corner room with velvet sky-blue curtains, a canopy bed with matching drapes and a mahogany dressing commode by Chippendale. Two sash windows faced the sweeping park.

"How pretty this room is!" She ran from window to window and looked out. Alas, there was no gardener in sight.

"Oh, Lucy, it is so wonderful to have you here! I can't tell you how boring it's been." Arabella pulled her to the middle of the room. "The house is full of people, but there isn't anyone with whom I share memories of the Seminary. I don't have anyone to talk to, except for Grandmama, who's as approachable as a hedgehog. And, oh, Ash, of course." Her face fell. "But he never has time for me."

Lucy's heart squeezed at the loneliness in her voice. "Do you remember those summer days when Miss Dempsey let us go to Sydney Gardens for drawing lessons because it was too hot in the classrooms? And we sat under the cool shades of the trees sketching flowers."

Arabella laughed. "And Pen absolutely loathed that, because she thought flowers were boring. She always tried to get away with drawing monstrous beetles and ants, but so realistically done she frightened Miss Dempsey. Remember how she screeched and dropped the drawing?"

The girls laughed.

"And how we used to get up at midnight and meet in Birdie's and Pen's room for a midnight snack. We'd bring our stack of sweets and biscuits and eat them as we told each other scary ghost stories." Lucy grinned.

"And then we'd be so tired the next day, we'd fall asleep in Mr Horatio's history class."

"But he never noticed because he was always so engrossed in his own storytelling."

Arabella's chuckle was low and pleasant. "Ah, Lucy, how I've missed those days."

Lucy hesitated, then confessed. "That's why I'm here. I want to go back. To teach."

"I thought there was more behind your story. Tell me." Arabella sat down on the bed and pulled her down next to her.

Lucy avoided her eyes. "I was a—governess for a while but it didn't turn out the way I imagined."

"What happened?"

"At first it wasn't so bad. The Grenville children were lovely. They seemed to like me, and I enjoyed teaching them. Can you imagine me as a governess?" Lucy chuckled. "So respectful and serious. I can be quite strict, you know. But I never had to punish them because they were good children and they learned fast."

"And then?"

Lucy's face darkened. "Then the oldest son returned from University and he decided he liked the way I looked."

"Oh no, Lucy! Did he assault you?" Arabella blanched.

"He tried, but I know how to defend myself." Lucy shook her fist. "I gave him a black eye." Arabella covered her mouth.

"They wouldn't believe I didn't encourage him. Everything was my fault. So, I packed up and left. Without references. I didn't even say goodbye to the children."

"Never mind the references," Arabella said. "But oh, what you must've suffered!" Her eyes brimmed with concern.

Lucy smiled bitterly. "I can take care of myself when I have to."

"I've always admired that about you, Lucy. Your strength and independence."

"Do you think Miss Hilversham will take me back?" Lucy's voice wobbled.

"Are you sure this is what you want? Now that you are here, I can help you find someone suitable to marry."

Lucy shook her head with determination. "No. I want to teach music and drama at the Seminary." She took Arabella's hands in hers. "I know you have forgiven me for the fiasco at the well. But do you think she has? Miss Hilversham. You know how she is."

Arabella nodded. "Strict and ferociously kind, yet more unyielding than iron. Oh, Lucy." She leaned her head against her shoulder. "If only I hadn't made those stupid wishes. I feel responsible for what happened. But knowing Miss Hilversham, she'll not change her mind unless something strong compels her to."

Lucy twisted her hands in her lap. "And if your brother writes to her? Would she change her mind, then?"

Arabella twisted her mouth in exasperation. "Oh, Ash. He's so stubborn! He's quite prejudiced against the school. He went from the biggest supporter of the school to biggest opposer. It won't be easy getting him to change his mind again."

Lucy exhaled, repressing the urge to say that her brother was unfortunately a numbskull.

"It's not only because of what happened," Arabella continued. "I think I made a mistake when I told him about all the fun we had with our pranks. He got the impression I learned nothing and wasted my time, which isn't true. He's so overprotective."

"He doesn't have to forgive me. But if I could only get him to reinstate his patronage, that would help tremendously." Lucy jumped up and paced.

Arabella rubbed her forehead. "I wish I could help you. But if I continue telling him how wonderful it's been and that the school is worth his sponsorship, and that he should change his mind, he'll just get more obnoxious. He can be so hard-headed sometimes." She pulled her lips to a rueful smile. "I suppose we Ashmores all are. It's a family trait."

"Your heads are certainly hard. Remember how loud the splash was when you and Pen crashed head-first into the well? Pen went in first, and you hung onto her, of all the silly things to do, for she dragged you down. I can't remember whose screech was louder. Yours or Pen's."

The girls looked at each other and burst out laughing.

Lucy returned to the bed and sat down. "Tell me about this Lord Finbar."

"It would be a very advantageous match." Arabella tugged at the drapery of the canopy.

"What's he like?"

Arabella thought for a while. "Beautiful."

"And?"

Arabella shrugged. "Beautiful."

"Aha. He's beautiful and beautiful. Sounds like an emptyheaded fop to me. He must be a terrible rake."

"I suppose so. He's a school friend of Ash. Most women rather like him. I think he likes them, too. He is very flirtatious with everyone."

"Do you want to marry a man like that?" Lucy looked at her closely.

Arabella hesitated.

"Do you love him?" Lucy prodded.

Arabella looked at the window with a far-away glance.

"You love someone else." It was a wild guess. But a rosy blush spread over Arabella's cheeks. Good heavens. Lucy bounced on the bed. "Who is he?"

Arabella covered her cheeks with her hands and jumped up. "Let's not talk about this. Or Finbar. Or love. Or marriage. Lucy. Please."

"But Arabella—" Lucy cut herself off at a tap on the door.

Meg entered and curtsied. She looked pale, but her eyes flashed with excitement. "I'm to be your abigail, Miss."

"Meg. I led you on a bit. Can you forgive me?" Lucy said with a slightly guilty look on her face.

"Miss, oh Miss. I couldn't believe it when I saw you sitting there with Her Grace. Poor John was beside himself when the tea tray was missing. I ran after you, but you were already in the drawing room. I waited outside, chewing my fingernails to the quick." Meg showed her maltreated fingernails.

"You must've been so shocked. Poor John. Did Mrs Bates scold him terribly?"

"She hadn't noticed yet."

"What an exciting life you seem to lead." Arabella looked at Meg curiously. She wasn't used to hearing such volubility pouring forth from the maids.

Meg curtsied again. "Yes, my Lady."

"I hope you can dress my hair, Meg." Lucy smiled to put her at ease.

"Yes, Miss, I can, am good at it, too. Used to dress my sisters' hair, and it was a lot longer than yours. I'm sorry, I'm so excited." She covered her face with her hands.

"Don't fret about it, Meg. It was my fault for not telling everyone who I am."

"I just wanted to say, thank you for helping me get this position!" Meg took Lucy's hand and kissed it.

"Don't be ridiculous, I'm not the queen. And you don't need to thank me. I know you're a hard worker."

"I'll never, ever forget your kindness. If only I'd known you were no housemaid—we're all so shocked! Mrs Bates fairly cried. I've never seen her cry!"

"Poor Mrs Bates. I never meant to make her cry!" She made a mental note to talk to Mrs Bates later.

"Oh no, look at the time! We have to get ready for dinner." Arabella opened the door to a mahogany clothes press. "Look. These dresses are either unworn or too small for me." She looked at Lucy anxiously. "We're the same height and nearly the same shape, though you're slimmer. I hope you don't mind taking my cast-offs?"

"Don't be silly, they're all gorgeous! But goodness, Arabella, what do I need so many dresses for?"

"Trust me, you will need them." She dug around and took out a sprigged muslin morning dress with green embroidered leaves and held it up to Lucy. "This used to be one of my favourites, but it's too small now. This green shawl here matches it nicely, and I think there's even a green-ribboned bonnet and matching kid slippers. I hope it fits you, otherwise I'll send you my maid to have it fixed. Oh, and this yellow dress here is a lovely afternoon dress for walking. And look here, a dinner gown." She shook out a cream silk and tulle gown with lace and embroidery at the hem.

Lucy had never worn anything as lovely as this. "Arabella, it's gorgeous."

"Try it on! In the meantime, I'll change my dress, too. Goodness, how time flies."

Arabella gave her a hug then left to her own quarters.

The evening dress fit Lucy perfectly.

Meg set to work and tied up Lucy's unruly curls in the current fashion.

"You look as lovely as any of the ladies, Miss. They already arrived. There's His Grace, together with the Duke of Tilbury and his daughter, Lady Louisa Whitehall. Then there are Lord and Lady Conway, and Lord and Lady Bleckingham with their daughter, Miss Jane Weston. There's to be picnics, concerts, and even a ball on Saturday."

Lucy groaned. "A ball." She couldn't imagine a worse way to spend the evening.

"It'll be wonderful, Miss, you'll see. His Grace rarely entertains, but when he does, it's always in big style."

Meg chattered on about the guests, while Lucy listened with growing discomfort. The duke didn't know she was here. Even with the Dowager Duchess's grudging acceptance of her and Arabella's support, Lucy doubted that he'd welcome her here. She'd try to keep in the background and wait for the opportunity when she could talk to the duke in private to ask for her letter. Then she'd leave. Preferably sooner rather than later.

CHAPTER 7

*L*ucy stood awkwardly in a corner in the drawing room, next to a big palm tree and wished she could be the tree. She hated nothing more than having to do small talk with a group of haughty people who looked down on her. When surrounded by elegant, judgmental ladies and arrogant dandies, she just could not be herself. None of her otherwise talkative, vivacious personality shone through. It was clear they shrugged her off as an insignificant, gauche girl.

Since neither the Dowager Duchess nor His Grace of Ashmore was present, the women circled around Arabella and Louisa.

Like vultures, Lucy thought.

A buxom lady in a mustard gown raised her quizzing glass at Lucy. "Bell. Never heard of them. As in the Durham Bells?"

"More likely the Sutherland Bells." Another pair of quizzing glasses, Lady Bleckingham's, fixated on Lucy.

"I'm not at all certain," replied Lady Conway, a fearful looking matron. "To my knowledge, the Sutherland Bells are not of a family of quality." Three coiffed heads turned to Lucy, who cringed even further into the palm tree. She felt like a pinned-down insect, inspected and categorised.

"Neither good breeding nor gentility, it appears." Lady Bleckingham sniffed. She was too tall and too thin to be beautiful but looked magnificent in silk and gold. A flush of shame shot through Lucy.

"Surely you are mistaken, Mama," said a gentle voice. "I daresay if she is Lady Arabella's friend, she must be in possession of gentility and good breeding." Lady Bleckingham's daughter, Jane, smiled apologetically at Lucy.

Lady Bleckingham dropped her quizzing glasses. "You are quite right, Jane. She must be of the Durham Bells. Somewhat impoverished family, but of good stock. It would be inconceivable of Ashmore, of all people, to tolerate anyone who is less than the best of quality to associate with his sister. He would never countenance it. He wouldn't care to be seen with such a person in the same room, least of all in the same house. I saw once how he cut—in a most magnificent manner—Harriet Westington when she tried to approach him in Drury Lane."

The group of women gasped collectively.

"You mean—*The* Harriet Westington?"

Lady Bleckingham nodded. "The actress. It is commonly known how His Grace would never deign to lower himself to talk to one of her kind." She bent forward and whispered, "So utterly unrespectable a person."

Lucy curled her lips and turned away. No wonder the Dowager Duchess didn't care for such conversations. She liked the dowager and disliked Arabella's brother somewhat more.

Arabella motioned for Lucy to join her. Lucy crossed the room, attempting not to stumble over her feet, relieved she had something to do, even if it was just walking across the room with half a dozen pairs of eyes on her.

"Lady Whitehall, may I present Miss Lucy Bell, my dearest friend. Miss Eloisa Stilton and her older sister, Miss Emma Stilton. They're Lady Rawleigh's nieces."

Everyone curtsied. The Stilton sisters looked like the two bad stepsisters from the fairy tale. One in garish pink, the other in baby blue, both with bad-tempered, haughty expressions.

But Lady Louisa Whitehall! Goodness, she was beautiful. White silk, white ribbons, white gloves, white satin slippers. Even her blonde hair was light to the border of being silver. She looked like a Meissen porcelain figurine that would be best stored in the china cupboard. Perfect, frail—and cold. So, this was to be the future Duchess of Ashmore. One could not account for tastes, but if the duke had a penchant for that type of woman, well. It wasn't any of her business.

Lady Louisa looked her up and down with watery pale eyes, and Lucy almost triumphed. Ha! Here was an imperfection! Her eyes were too light for warmth, and she had short eyelashes and no eyebrows at all. Her forehead was revoltingly smooth, like a skull.

"How do you do." Lady Louisa barely nodded at her and then turned back to her conversation with two other ladies, who did likewise. It was not exactly rude behaviour, as they had greeted her, but she still felt snubbed. Suddenly, she was tired of being ignored.

"I've some indigestion but otherwise I'm fine, thank you. I probably just need to get more fresh air. Take a walk. Did you enjoy your walk in the wet grass at the Abbey?" She flashed a bright smile at them.

Lady Louisa, who'd considered her interaction with Lucy to be over, turned her head in astonishment. "Walk?"

"Indeed." Lucy nodded. "It's so very good for one's

complexion. I daresay you could do with some more fresh air as you seem rather white around the mouth."

"I beg your pardon?" If looks could freeze, Lucy would be an ice statue now.

"They say fresh air brings some healthy colour to one's face."

"So one ends up looking like a farm girl?" Louisa twisted her mouth into a line of disdain.

"That's always better than having the hue of a corpse, don't you think?" Lucy put on an innocent look.

The trio gasped.

Arabella's laughter trilled into the awkward pause. "Lucy and I, we love to walk. There's nothing better than a natural blush and not having to pinch one's cheeks to get them to look red."

"Quite so, Lady Arabella. However, one wouldn't want to overdo it. It is neither genteel nor attractive to have the reddish complexion of a farmer's help. This afternoon's walk," Louisa wrinkled her dainty white porcelain nose, "was already quite *de trop*. I ruined my new satin slippers."

"Oh, I always take along my sunshade," Arabella said cheerfully. "A shame I couldn't join you on the outing to the Abbey, but you know, my headache." She pulled Lucy away.

"Am I white around my mouth?" Louisa asked the other girls.

Lucy stifled a giggle.

"She's like that with everyone. They're somewhat exclusive." Arabella took her arm and walked her to another group. Exclusive! Lucy somehow doubted it. Snobbish was more like it.

"Oh, I wish the men would return from their hunting," Miss Stilton, the one in the garish pink dress, exclaimed.

"It is quite a bore that His Grace isn't present—again—for supper." Viscountess Rawleigh's enormous purple plume sticking in her turban almost touched the chandeliers when she walked underneath them.

"I daresay he has pressing matters to see to. He is such a busy man." Aside from Arabella, Miss Jane Weston seemed to be the only sympathetic woman in the entire room.

Lucy couldn't help but feel relieved that the duke wasn't here.

"Lucy?" She turned at Arabella's voice.

"Lucy, may I present Lord Finbar? Finbar, this is my friend Lucy Bell."

He was, as Arabella had said, beautiful. He looked like a Greek statue, with a head full of unruly golden curls, limpid green eyes and a sensual mouth drawn up in a charming smile. He was dressed in a silver grey topcoat and high shirt points that nearly stuck into his cheeks.

"Enchanted." He lifted her hand and breathed a kiss on the back.

"I've known Lucy since we were at the Seminary together."

"Lady Arabella's friends are my friends." His vapid smile never reached his eyes.

What a vain dolt, Lucy thought.

"What do you say to this house party, Miss Bell? Charming, is it not? Ashmore and Lady Arabella do their best to entertain us. This afternoon we went to Kloster Abbey. Alas, you missed it. It was charming. Tomorrow we shall ride to those ruins—I forget their name—they're said to be utterly gorgeous—medieval romance with a touch of decay—you'll join us, and you'll love it, yes?"

"I'm not sure—"

"Of course you'll join us, Lucy. I won't allow you to stay behind on your own."

Lord Finbar pulled up the corners of his lips. "Unless it rains. Alas. How much it rained this summer. Then we'll remain here and play baccarat. Or charades. Or whatever game our charming Lady Arabella devises for us." He bowed to Arabella. "Such lovely games! But also the Lady Louisa Whitehall has some charming ideas." His glance flitted over to the porcelain doll.

Poor Arabella. Lucy wondered how she could bear marrying this man, especially when she was in love with someone else. But who could it be? Lucy vowed to find out.

THE NEXT MORNING, LUCY CREPT OUT OF THE HOUSE AFTER breakfast to search for Henry. Yes, he'd said they should not meet again. But she desperately needed to know how Bartimaeus was doing. She also needed to ask him whether he'd found his horse, carriage and the bushes. And to check whether his eyes were still that lovely, clear and steady shade of blue, whether the smell of the mix of tobacco and grass still hung on to his clothes.

A longing washed over her like she'd never known before. It was a feverish homesickness that burned slowly and left her restless. *How odd,* Lucy thought. *I'm homesick for a person I've only known for two days.* The intenseness of the feeling took her breath away.

She went to the stables to seek Bartimaeus. A fellow who shovelled hay directed to a corner where a little boy was playing with several adorable puppies. But Bartimaeus was not there.

"Hello there," she said, startling the boy.

He looked at her defiantly. "I no doin' no wrong."

"Of course you're not." Lucy knelt next to him on the floor and watched the little puppies. "I'm looking for a puppy, too. But mine is black and only has three legs. You haven't seen her, have you?"

The boy shook his head. He couldn't be older than five.

He tilted his dirty face towards her and looked at her suspiciously.

Lucy smiled involuntarily. "What's your name?"

"Jem."

"Jem. That's a pretty name."

"I's hungry."

Lucy's heart constricted. "Of course you are, Jem." She got up. "They don't feed you enough, do they?"

"Jimmy forgets."

"Who's Jimmy?"

"Brother. Lamp boy."

"So he is." She recalled seeing a rumpled-looking boy frantically refilling the lamps at the bottom of the back stairs. She'd nearly fallen over him. He'd had a tear-stained face because Higgins, the butler, had scolded him for having tipped over a lamp and the oil had smeared the parquet floor. Being scolded by Higgins was like being scolded by royalty. To a servant boy, it must be the most terrifying thing imaginable. The only thing more terrifying than that was to be noticed by the duke. Lucy frowned. Jimmy the lamp boy was one thing. But his little brother Jem, alone and hungry in the stables? That wouldn't do.

"And your mummy? Or daddy?"

The boy just looked at her with huge, hungry eyes.

"Right. Well then," Lucy got up and shook her skirts, "let's see what we can find you to eat."

She procured a plate filled with a fruit scone, a triangular cucumber sandwich and a slice of seed cake directly from the cook. As a former housemaid-turned-lady, Lucy was now a celebrity below stairs, and she could get anything she wanted from them.

Lucy took the plate back to the stables and watched Jem eat. He was so tiny.

The boy looked at her with a forlorn expression when she

left. She made a mental note to instruct the cook to feed the boy properly.

She thought of going into the forest to look for Henry. But her morning dress was not appropriate for a forest walk. Arabella would wonder where she was. But there was still enough time for her to look for some kind of toy. For Jem.

"I'll be back soon," she promised.

After nuncheon, Lucy went searching for toys. Arabella had suggested the old nursery, but Lucy only found a handful of marbles in the drawer of a Chinese cabinet.

She walked into the blue salon, counting the marbles in her hand. She didn't look up until she was already in the room.

"Arabella, I've found only five marbles, and two of them are chipped and useless. No idea where the others are. Do you think they might be in the attic somewhere?"

She looked up and saw that Arabella was not alone but having tea with the guests. With a little smile, Arabella indicated her to turn around.

"What?" Lucy tilted her head. She'd not seen the tall, stern man standing by the fireplace, his hands clasped behind his back.

"Here she is, Ash. I'm so pleased to present my friend Lucy Bell. Lucy, this is my brother, the Duke of Ashmore. Finally, you two get to meet!"

A wave of shock slapped her.

She heard her own quick, sharp intake of breath as she stared into Henry's steel blue eyes.

CHAPTER 8

"*M* iss Bell." The duke gave her a dismissive nod.

She reeled. A buzzing started in her ears. With pounding heart, Lucy dropped into an automatic, lop-sided curtsy. Her fingers clenched around her marbles, crunching them together.

I better not drop them now, was the only thought in her mind.

Someone said something, but the roaring din in her ears wouldn't stop. She felt like she was underwater, and voices no longer sounded like normal voices but like they came from a bubble. And she was outside of that bubble, looking in. People moved their mouths, but she didn't comprehend what they said. The duke must have addressed her, because everyone looked at her in expectation.

The words were wedged in her throat. "Uh—I'm sorry." Her legs gave way, and she plopped down on the chaise longue next to the Dowager Duchess. Never mind that she was breaking social etiquette since no one had invited her to sit in the presence of the duke. For sit she would. In the worst case, she'd sit on the floor. Disoriented, she looked at Arabella for help. Arabella's face was full of concern.

The duke looked on with an air of utter boredom, as if the answer to his question didn't matter.

"Losing the ability to hear is my prerogative," the Dowager Duchess informed Lucy with a sniff. Then, directed at her grandson, "I am sure everything is in good order, and her rooms are to her liking."

"Oh, y–yes." Lucy stuttered. If she gripped the marbles any harder, she'd crush them to glass dust. Hushed tittering came from a group of women who stood by the window.

"Where were we?" The Dowager Duchess thumped her stick on the floor. "Ah yes. That infernal ball. Ashmore, I insist that you organise a proper orchestra. One that can read notes properly. The one you had the last time was an insult to all musical ears. I cannot bear to suffer through it another time, nor can anyone with a little sense of musicality in their body."

"Whatever you wish, Grandmama. I will instruct Brown to hire musicians from the Philharmonic Society." His familiar, deep voice gave her goosebumps, but the unutterably bored drawl with which he uttered this reply alienated her.

It was all a colossal mistake, Lucy thought. This was not Henry. This man was the Duke of Ashmore, the embodiment of the arrogant aristocrat. He was a haughty marble statue. The highest form of emotion he knew was one of boredom.

He was polished from top to toe, impeccably dressed in topcoat, skin-tight breeches and Hessians. There was not a single crease on him. His dark hair, slicked back, revealed a proud forehead and high cheekbones. Thus, his nose was in a sharp profile. He had the same eagle-like nose as the Dowager Duchess. The colour of his eyes was the same as Arabella's. She didn't know why she hadn't seen that before.

His lips were thin, proud, and entirely humourless. Those lips had never smiled, nor joked in their entire life.

"Well done, Ashmore, they say the Philharmonics are first-rate, the world's best musicians," said a whiskered gentleman in a colonel's uniform, whose name Lucy had forgotten.

"Not so," the gentle voice of Mr Fridolin spoke up. He was an elderly gentleman with a shock of white hair. "I need to protest. That status no doubt belongs to the Viennese musicians. They're incomparable."

"Fiddlesticks," interjected the Dowager Duchess.

"I say, Ashmore. That's all well and good, to have this splendid ball with England's best musicians. Wouldn't expect anything less of you. But, dash it, no point in having a ball if half of the time you're absent. 'Tis not the thing," said an overweight, ruddy-looking gentleman. He tapped his snuff box open and took a pinch.

"Lord Blackmore is right, Ash." Arabella said. "You've been neglecting your guests."

"How is it to be the grandest ball in the country, if you're absent, sir?" Lady Louisa pulled her porcelain face into a pout.

The duke proved marble could stiffen. "I regret my tardiness this week. It is indeed inexcusable for a host to desert his guests. There were unforeseen and not untrivial complications on the estate. I shall make amends. You will not lack in comfort and amusement for your remaining stay at Ashmore Hall."

Good heavens. He even talked like he'd eaten marble.

"Very well said, Ashmore." Lord Blackmore was satisfied. "We all know what a busy man you are. Wouldn't want to shoulder half the troubles and responsibilities you have. But now is some time for sport and fun, eh?"

"I shall make every effort to oblige you, Blackmore." The

duke looked about as amused and capable of having fun as an urn. "Lady Louisa, of course I will attend the ball." He bowed in her direction. "It would be an honour if you were to grant me the first dance."

"Wonderful!" Louisa clapped her gloved hands together with spread fingers, like a child.

"Yes, yes. On to more important matters," grumbled the dowager. "Tea!"

The men gathered around Ashmore to discuss the newest politics of the day. The women gathered around Louisa to discuss what they'd wear for the ball. The footmen brought in tea trays.

Lucy exhaled shakily. She felt cold, yet there were beads of sweat on her forehead.

"Are you well, Lucy? You don't seem quite yourself." Arabella bent over her as she handed Lucy a cup of tea. "You're white around your nose. But now your cheeks are red, they look feverish. For a moment I thought you'd faint."

"I almost did. The air in here is stifling. A moment of vertigo, nothing else." Lucy swallowed the tea without tasting it.

"Are you ill?" Arabella tilted her head sideways and looked at her closely. Lucy shook her head. "Maybe you just need some fresh air. Did you not say you wanted to go to the rose garden and take a walk? How about after tea?"

"No. I'm tired. I need to lie down a bit."

Arabella wanted to reply, when Lady Conway tapped her arm and drew her away.

His eyes. Icy blue. Cold and indifferent. She must have imagined they could lighten up in a million shades of blue when he smiled. Or she must have been completely, entirely mistaken.

The things she'd told him! How he must have laughed at her. And she'd kissed him!

Humiliation flushed through her body. Her eyes burned with unshed tears. She swore to herself she'd forevermore hate hawthorn bushes, roses, and gardeners.

How was she going to get through tea? It was turning into an agonisingly drawn-out affair. She could excuse herself and return to her room. She set her teacup aside. Just at that moment, the steely grip of the dowager clamped down on her arm.

"Ashmore." Stomp, stomp. "There's a matter of great importance that has been brought to my attention. Sit down here. No, not there. Over here." The dowager pointed with her stick to the ottoman across from where she sat with Lucy.

The duke folded his tall figure into the ottoman and crossed his long legs. "Grandmama."

"Were you aware of the fact that our domestic staff each have appellations?"

"Do they, now?" He raised a supercilious eyebrow.

"An indomitable source of information has informed me that our servants are not only people, but that they also have their very own names."

Ashmore's eyes, now with both brows raised, rested on Lucy, who found the green paisley pattern of the wallpaper intensely interesting. "Indeed, Grandmama. I find this indomitable source of information interests me profoundly. What else does he—or she— have to say?"

"It appears we've been shockingly remiss in this matter."

"How quaint," interjected Lady Louisa. "Servants are servants. One need not recognise them as individuals, as we all know. In our house, all footmen are called John, and all chambermaids Mary. It simplifies the matter tremendously." She sat down next to the duke, holding a teacup, looking cool in a pristine white gown with a pink satin sash.

Something in Lucy snapped. "But what do you do when

you have more than one chambermaid called Mary?" Thankfully, she'd found her tongue again.

"I do not understand your question, Miss Bell. What does it matter if there is one, or many?" Lady Louisa took a dainty sip from her porcelain cup.

"Do you call them Mary One, Mary Two and Mary Three?" Lucy found a perverse pleasure in challenging her. "Mary Three, bring me my pelisse. Mary Two, not the pink walking shoes but the green ones. Mary One, a cup of hot chocolate, if you please. Wait. Actually, I meant Mary Two, after she finishes with my wardrobe. Or was it Mary Three I meant?"

"Jolly good, heheheh." Blackmore chortled.

Lady Louisa gave her a look of intense dislike. "I just call them all plain Mary. Or most of the time, nothing at all. What does it matter? I do not see where the issue lies. How shocking to be conversing with domestics to begin with." She helped herself to a pink meringue, which she held daintily between two fingers. She'd eat it without dropping a single crumb.

"Yonder footman over there. Can you attach a name to him?" Lucy pointed at the footman who stood at attention by the door. She stared hard at the duke. "Your Grace?"

The duke looked at the footman perplexed, as if only now aware of his presence. "What is your name?"

"John, Your Grace," he replied with a bow.

"Very sensible name," Lady Louisa approved.

"Your real name," Lucy insisted.

"Felix Xaver Zornmann, Your Grace."

"There. You see?" Lady Louisa pulled a face. "It is entirely unpronounceable. Besides, you can't possibly call a footman Felix Xaver."

"'Tis not the thing," agreed Blackmore.

"Are you of German origin, Felix?" the Dowager Duchess asked.

"Yes, Your Grace."

"Aha! Now we know two things about our first footman, Ashmore. His name is Felix, and his parents are from Prussia." The dowager leaned back, satisfied.

"Really, Grandmama. Why this unanticipated interest in the identity of our domestics?" Ashmore crossed his arms.

"Because it amuses me. Besides, we're to show more attentiveness towards our fellow human beings. By tomorrow, Ashmore, you're to rattle off the correct appellations of all our hundred or so domestics and assign the right faces to them. Including the stable boy. No exception."

"Undoubtedly I have nothing better to do with my time." A shadow of annoyance crossed his face. "Any other recommendation from that indomitable source of information as to how I should run my house and estate?"

"Raise their salaries." It popped out of Lucy's mouth before she could help herself. She quickly took a big gulp of tea, emitting an unladylike slurp.

The dowager cackled.

Lady Louisa looked shocked.

Felix Xaver's face brightened.

"Not at all the thing, not at all the thing," quipped Blackmore.

The duke pressed his lips together in a disapproving, humourless line. Heaven help her. Only a day ago she'd kissed those lips!

He narrowed his eyes. "Pray what are you clutching in your hands, Miss Bell?" he asked.

"Er. Nothing." She gave him a wide-eyed look.

"This nothing seems to emit crunching noises," the duke observed.

That was because Lucy's hands were sweaty and her

crushing grip on the marbles caused them to shift about with a crunching noise. There again, a crunch.

He lifted an eyebrow.

She straightened her spine and glared back. Any minute now the hot ball somersaulting in her stomach would explode. And then she'd demand an explanation why he ran around as gardener Henry. Why he deceived her so cruelly.

His expression stilled. There was a warning in his eyes. He shook his head. It was so subtle, maybe she'd imagined it.

He didn't want her to acknowledge that they knew each other in public. She exhaled shakily.

"Marbles," she blurted out. "It's marbles."

"Of course it is," the Dowager Duchess said as she helped herself to her third canape. "When in doubt, it must be the marbles."

"Marbles." The duke looked baffled. Lucy choked back a laugh. For one second, she'd broken through his aloofness. Could she do so again? Was her Henry underneath that abominable veneer after all?

She opened her hand and showed him her treasure.

Blackmore looked at them through his quizzing glass. "Blimey. They're marbles all right."

"How quaint." Lady Louisa looked like she'd never seen marbles in her entire life. "They're boys' toys, are they not?"

The duke stared at the marbles. Not a muscle in his face twitched as he said, "They're indeed boys' toys. And if I am not mistaken, they're mine. I seem to recall they were my favourite." He held out his hand. Lucy dropped the sweaty glass balls into his palm. She could not imagine the duke ever playing with marbles.

"I didn't know they were yours, sir. I thought if no one needed them, I'd take them."

"You mean to say you play with marbles, Miss Bell, do you, by Jove?" Blackmore's beady eyes twinkled.

"How unladylike!" interjected Lady Louisa.

"I intended to give them to Jimmy."

The duke sighed. "I dare not ask who this Jimmy is." He raised a hand. "Spare me the lecture. He is no doubt either the bootblack or the stable boy."

"He is the lamp boy."

"Ah. I was close. And why would he need marbles when this Jimmy ought to occupy his time refilling my lamps?"

"They're not for him but for his younger brother, Jem, who is only five. Their mother died recently, you see, and Jimmy's raising him alone. He's not yet eleven. Jem is mostly in the stables getting into mischief. I thought I could give him the marbles to keep him busy."

"Miss Bell. You seem to have made a very intimate acquaintance with my serving staff in such a short amount of time."

He had no idea. It was a shocking and unladylike thing to have done, her stint as a housemaid. And it certainly was not considered appropriate for people of their station to consort with servants.

"Wonderful, Ashmore. I see we're improving. Next to the Prussian Felix, you have a lamp boy called Jimmy who has a brother called Jem." The dowager was enjoying herself tremendously. "In due course we shall no doubt learn the identities of the chimney sweep, accompanied by his entire family history. It is vastly entertaining."

Lady Louisa looked back and forth in bewilderment. "Can we really be discussing lamp boys and chimney sweeps?"

The duke leaned back and looked at Lucy with hooded eyes. One long finger stirred the marbles in his palm. Then he held them out to her. Their fingers brushed lightly, and Lucy almost jerked her hand back at the spark between them. He dropped the marbles into her palm, slowly, one by one.

"You may give them to this Jem, Miss Bell," he murmured, giving Lucy goosebumps.

"Thank you." She sagged. She couldn't maintain this for much longer.

"Well. How very quaint." Lady Louisa shook her head in amazement. "Now that this is done, may we discuss how we shall spend the evening? How about charades, or a round of spillikins?"

"Whatever you wish, Lady Louisa," the duke replied with a bored voice, but he looked at Lucy as if she posed him an unsolvable riddle. This irked her, because it should be the other way around. He puzzled her. He owed her an explanation. Why? The duke ignored her questioning gaze as he retreated once more behind his aloofness.

"I prefer a round of whist myself," Blackmore's voice boomed. "Finbar? Bleckingham? Who else is in?"

"Not for me, thank you. I will peruse the library, if His Grace doesn't mind. I've seen you have a notable collection of music there." Mr Fridolin looked at the duke expectantly.

"My dear Fridolin, we shall look forward to your professional opinion on our collection," the duke replied.

"I shall join the ladies with spillikins," the gentle voice of Mr Gabriel interjected. "If the ladies allow."

"Splendid, Mr Gabriel." Arabella's face brightened, and Mr Gabriel smiled at her. Lucy made a mental note to investigate this Mr Gabriel. Was he the one Arabella was in love with?

"I see the evening's entertainment tonight is over for me." The dowager pulled herself up on her cane. "Neither whist nor spillikins nor heaven forbid, charades, tempt me." She shuddered. "I will retire."

The duke got up. "I'll see you to your room."

"But you'll return, will you not, Your Grace?" Lady Louisa's voice sounded whiny.

"The whist, Your Grace!"

"I'll return imminently. Gentlemen. Ladies." He gave a curt nod in their direction. Lucy scrambled up. The ladies curtsied in unison, Lucy missed the moment and tagged on a hasty curtsy, and he left the room with the dowager.

"In other words, he's off for another hour or two to work and then maybe he'll remember he has guests. I wouldn't count on him until tomorrow afternoon," said Blackmore. "Gentlemen, the cards await."

Lady Louisa pouted. She got up and joined the ladies by the window.

"Odd girl," Lucy heard her say. "Excessively odd. Marbles indeed."

"Yet he talked to her for over half an hour. She undoubtedly tried to flirt with him." The Stilton girls giggled. Louisa frowned.

It doesn't matter what the others think; Lucy told herself fiercely. None of it mattered a whit. Least of all him.

Yet, back in her room, she threw herself on the bed and cried her eyes out over a man she'd found and lost.

CHAPTER 9

*L*ucy didn't want to go to a drawn-out supper and face him again. She thought of excusing herself with a headache, but that seemed cowardly. And Lucy Bell was anything but a coward.

She took particular care with her appearance. She put on an ivory taffeta gown with lace trim that the maid had adjusted for her. Her grey eyes glowed and nervousness brought a red tinge to her cheeks.

"How pretty you look, Lucy," Arabella told her. She looked fetching in a pale lemon-yellow gown.

Lucy's insides quivered as she descended the stairs and the conversation lulled as all heads turned towards the girls. Lucy flushed. She located the duke who stood, clad in dark blue, beside the fireplace, talking with Lady Louisa. He appeared, Lucy thought with some gratification, bored as usual. Their eyes met, and she looked away quickly. It was too hot in the room even though her dress had short sleeves.

She would try her best to ignore him, which ought not to be too difficult as surely at dinner she would be seated far away from him, being of such minor social significance. If only her heart would stop thudding so violently.

"Charming, how charming," Lord Finbar drawled, looking from one to the other as if at a loss, then remembered his manners and kissed Arabella's hand first, before bowing over Lucy's. His lips were warm and wet.

"Like spring flowers. What a sight for sore eyes." She pulled her hand away.

"There you are. What a spectacle you two girls make entering together. You are quite outshining the rest of them." The dowager looked splendid in silver from top to toe. "I daresay the gentlemen are making oaf eyes already. I know at least one lady who will not be pleased. It'll be an amusing evening. Finbar, I see you have found your table partner already. Fridolin," she turned to the tall, thin man who hovered behind her, "you will take Miss Bell to dinner."

Lucy hadn't expected this. As Mr Fridolin's partner, she was seated in closer proximity to the head of the table than she felt comfortable. She couldn't hide behind the flower arrangement but had to converse reasonably coherently, within Ashmore's earshot.

At the head of the table sat Ashmore, unsmiling, eating rapidly with little enjoyment. Lucy recalled with what gusto Henry had bitten into the loaf of farmer's bread, and how he'd held one piece in one hand, and a piece of cheese in the other, leaning both elbows on the table and wiping his mouth with his sleeve. His mussed hair had fallen over his eyes, which had never left her face. The memory tugged at her heart. Ashmore, however, sat stiffly, not touching the chair's back, and handled his fork and knife with precision.

Lucy watched, fascinated, how his finger ran up and down the stem of his wineglass. He picked the glass up and looked over its rim. Their eyes locked.

Her stomach turned into a buzzing beehive. Heavy eyelids fell over his languid gaze, leaving her hot and shaken.

Lucy gawked at him, the fork dangling from her hand. Possibly, she was drooling.

"Miss Bell?"

Lucy tore her glance away and saw Fridolin look at her with amusement.

"I have been asking twice already whether you like music?"

"Oh yes, I find it enjoyable," she answered mechanically. Lady Louisa touched the duke's sleeve with her gloved hand, and Lucy gripped her knife.

Mr Fridolin loaded his fork with string beans. "I mean beyond the occasional drawing room lullaby or amateurish piano recital. I'm a great fan of music, particularly opera. And the concerts are a delight. Ah, Vienna. The music there is incomparable. Beethoven, for example. Though I understand the mediocre ear might consider his music to be rather incomprehensible." No doubt he expected Lucy to have such a mediocre ear.

"I am acquainted with his music."

Fridolin smiled knowingly. "Pray, tell me which of his musical compositions is your favourite?"

Sensing he was testing her, Lucy answered carefully. "The Seventh Symphony."

"You surprise me. I would have expected a more conventional answer from a lady like you. The Moonlight Sonata, perhaps. And which movement would you say is the most pleasing to your ears?"

"The Allegretto is most impressive. I cried the first time I heard it in London."

"Ah and help my rather rusty old mind. That was which movement?" He looked at her expectantly, setting his fork down.

"The Symphony has four movements. The Allegretto is the second one." Lucy popped her fork into her mouth.

Fridolin crowed, which caused the heads to turn in their directions. "What an unexpected delight to encounter a young person as yourself to be so well conversant in music. You have received a most excellent musical education, I gather? With a private tutor?"

"At Miss Hilversham's Seminary in Bath. Yes, she engaged only the best teachers for us. My teacher was Herr Hildebrand. He was from Vienna, like you."

"Oh, Lucy is excellent in music. And in geometry," Arabella spoke up from across the table. "She outdid all of us in those subjects." Arabella beamed at Lucy, whereby she accomplished what Lucy wanted to avoid: having all attention on her.

"Nonsense, Arabella," Lucy mumbled. "I remember you were not so bad at arithmetic yourself."

"What, what. Geometry and young ladies? Is that proper?" Blackmore interjected in between two bites of roast beef.

"Why ever not? My mind is capable of geometry as much as yours." Lucy frowned.

Blackmore's eyes lit up at the challenge. "Oho. Let us test that geometric mind of yours, Miss Bell. Tell me. How much is the ratio of a circle's circumference to its diameter?"

All eyes were on Lucy. She felt only one pair that truly mattered, and sensed, rather than saw, him raise his eyebrow in amused anticipation of an answer. However, Blackmore didn't give her time to reply. Certain that she didn't know the answer, he said, "Not many know that the correct answer is 3.14148. Also known as Archimedes constant, represented by the Greek letter pi." He chuckled and wiped his greasy lips on his napkin.

"3.14159," Lucy countered.

"Eh?"

"The circle's circumference to its diameter is a common fraction: 22/7. The correct answer is 3.14159." Lucy blessed Mr Hobb, who'd made them memorise pi to all five decimal places.

The gentlemen scrambled to calculate in their minds. Arabella was the first to nod at Lucy in agreement.

"Dash it. Is that correct?" Lord Conway gave up.

"She is correct." The duke's crisp voice came from the top of the table.

"A lady who is not only conversant in music but also in geometry. How impressive." Mr Fridolin beamed at Lucy.

Lady Louisa sniffed. "How entirely over-educated. Whatever is the use of knowing that piece of information? One will be mistaken for a bluestocking and be rendered forevermore unmarriageable."

"I do not see the contradiction. On the contrary. An arithmetical mind might come in useful in a marriage." Lucy sensed, too late, that she should not have picked up the gauntlet.

"Pray enlighten us, Miss Bell. I am fairly agog to know in what sense an arithmetical mind is useful in a marriage." This was the languid voice of the duke.

Lucy dabbed the corner of her mouth with a napkin, self-conscious that his eyes were on her lips. "Household accounts." She shrugged.

"I would have my steward do that." Lady Louisa looked down her nose. "Or my housekeeper."

"And who oversees your steward and your housekeeper? Do you do so, Your Grace?"

"I trust my secretary to do the job."

"Yes. But how economical if, at a glance, you could do so yourself and not be forevermore depending on strangers to do the job."

"That depends on the reliability and trustworthiness of those strangers." He toyed with his glass.

"And their honesty and entire lack of duplicity. I find not too many people have those qualities." Why did she have the feeling they were no longer talking about arithmetic?

"Touché." He lifted his glass and a slight smile played about his lips.

There was silence and puzzled gazes as the remaining guests attempted to follow their conversation.

"Fiddlesticks," the dowager said. "It is not a shame for a woman to have a head on her shoulders that she might take advantage of once in a while. Having come to this momentous conclusion, I suggest we turn to a more pressing pastime: pudding." She signalled the footmen to bring in ices, trifles, candied fruits and tarts decorated with sugar-paste.

Lucy's gaze remained locked with the duke's. Flushing, she tore her eyes away.

For there was something decidedly smouldering in his stare.

CHAPTER 10

*T*he next day, the gentlemen went out shooting. The ladies remained behind, embroidering or walking in the gardens.

Lucy could have screamed with frustration and boredom. She couldn't bear sitting in the drawing room, listening to their gossip. She'd rather clear out fireplaces. Her legs felt like there were invisible ants crawling up and down them, and she kept tapping her toes on the floor to shake them off. Her pulse beat erratically every time she thought of the duke. On top of being angry at him, she was annoyed at herself for wanting to burst into tears every time she thought of Henry. The gardener. Not the duke. Confound it. How confused she was! She'd jabbed her thumb as she tried to embroider, and now the silk was smeared with blood.

Lucy threw down the embroidery frame, jumped up, and decided to look for little Bart. Where could she be? She asked Felix the footman in the hall.

"She has her basket in the duke's study, Miss," he replied.

In the study! Now that she didn't expect.

"Miss. I know it's not my place, but on behalf of the

servants here, thank you for your intercession the other day. No one has ever asked for a pay increase on our behalf. You are our very own heroine now."

Lucy blushed and waved it away. "Nonsense, Felix."

"I thought you would like to know that cook will send you a special treat. If there is anything you ever need from us, you need but ask."

"Make sure Jimmy and Jem are always well-fed."

"Yes, Miss. They will receive the best from the kitchen."

Lucy smiled. "Thank you, Felix."

He bowed and left.

Lucy waited until he turned the corner, then she whisked across the corridor.

The duke's study was located in another wing. She'd never been there.

Lucy speculated if she should go there. He spent more time in his study than out of it. Yet she knew he was out riding with the male guests. She could feign a headache and, coincidentally, explore his study.

It took her a while until she found the study. It was a male domain, filled with evidence that serious work happened there. There were bookshelves stuffed with books that looked heavily used. His desk was disorderly and covered with piles of paper.

A familiar pipe rested in a black marble stand next to a pile of paper. It was the same pipe he'd handed to her. She brushed it with a finger. Something flooded through her, wrapping tightly around her heart like hot lead, taking her breath away.

Henry and the duke. She could not reconcile the two. It was impossible. Why did he lead this double life? Why the charade? Who was the real person? The duke? The gardener?

Could both be real? She didn't understand anything anymore.

A yipping came from under the desk.

"Bartimaeus," Lucy murmured.

Little Bart came hopping towards her and fell over her legs in excitement. She picked up the little pup and pressed kisses into her soft fur.

"Oh, my little one, how are you?"

Lucy found a gnawed-on little stick tucked away in the basket. Lucy tossed it, and Bart stumbled after it with a high-pitched yelp. She fell on her nose several times but returned with the stick, refusing to give it up. Lucy laughed as she tugged on it.

"You need to be trained, little miss."

Bart yelped, then rolled on her back, sticking her little legs into the air. Lucy scratched her soft pink tummy. Then she heard firm footsteps in the corridor, and male voices approaching.

Lucy blanched. She'd forgotten about the time. The duke was coming, and he would catch her sitting on the floor playing with the puppy. There was no time to flee. There was only time to hide. Her eyes darted around hectically. The cabinet? Too small. The curtains? Too obvious. The footsteps stopped in front of the door. Too late.

She dove under the desk.

Little Bart, thinking it was a fun game, barked, and followed her.

The desk was massive, so there was enough space for her underneath to curl up in one corner, behind Bart's basket. It had a wooden board on the bottom, so they would not see her from the other side.

"Shh," she mumbled. Little Bart bit playfully on her fingers and rolled up in her lap as the door opened and someone entered the room.

"I have papers here explaining these figures." The voice seemed to belong to his secretary, Brown.

"Excellent. I want you to examine them and take notes. Report on the newest developments now. We have half an hour until supper."

"Yes, Your Grace."

The footsteps came closer and Lucy held her breath. The chair was pulled aside, and she saw a pair of shiny Hessians.

He sat down and crossed his legs. One of his feet dangled in front of her nose. If he moved his foot, he'd touch the tip of her nose. He had big feet, long and narrow. She supposed that made sense since he was a tall man. Back when he was gardener Henry, she'd not noticed because he'd always hunched.

Bart yipped. The duke lowered his hand. He evidently expected Bart to come to him, so Lucy pushed him forward.

Mr Brown droned on and rattled off figures, and Ashmore scratched Bart's ears. Lucy watched his long fingers hypnotically.

Listening to the duke conduct his affairs with his secretary was soporific. She suppressed a yawn.

Then, Mr Brown's chair scraped on the floor and his footsteps sounded across the room. The door opened and closed. He'd left.

She held her breath. What was Ashmore waiting for?

She heard the leather crunch in the chair as he leaned back and crossed his legs. He took his pipe, lit it, and the smell of tobacco wafted through the air.

Lucy stopped breathing.

Any moment now she would sneeze.

She held her nose and suppressed it. Relieved when she didn't make a sound, Lucy slumped against the desk.

It took him forever to finish smoking. She heard the

clank of the pipe on the ashtray. He pushed his chair back with a creak.

"I trust you've made yourself comfortable underneath my desk, Miss Bell," he said. "No doubt you'll venture forth in your own time."

The game was over.

Lucy scrambled out with a scarlet face.

He didn't look in the least surprised to see her there.

"How did you know?"

"There is a certain smell of fresh wildflowers that seems to cling to your person. Since there are no flowers in the room, I concluded it must be you. No one else has that precise smell." He crossed his arms and studied her. "It is a mix of *glebionis segetum* and *malva moschata*."

Lucy stared at him. What on earth was he talking about?

"Marigold and musk mallow," he clarified.

"I just wanted to see Bartimaeus." She tilted her chin up. She had every right to see Bart.

"Undoubtedly. And also test her basket? Does its softness meet your approval?"

"She has a nice little place here. At least she isn't lonely."

The duke put the puppy back in the basket. "You had best leave before Brown returns."

"Yes." She straightened her spine and walked to the door with stiff, measured steps. Then she turned. "Why?" she blurted out.

"Why what?"

"Why did you not tell me who you were?"

The duke glanced at the door. "Now is not the time to discuss this. Brown will return momentarily."

"Did you enjoy yourself? Did you make fun of me, laugh at me, when you listened to all my stories that were meant for Henry the gardener?" Her eyes burned with unshed tears.

He frowned, but she didn't give him a chance to speak.

"I would have trusted Henry with my life. But you?" She hated that her voice wobbled.

"Lucy—" His jaw tightened. He got up and towered above her.

Lucy shook her head and backed off. "I don't know you. I don't know who you are." She rushed to the door, tore it open, and darted out. She bumped into an astonished Mr Brown, who nearly dropped a pile of documents. "Drat the man."

"I—I most sincerely apologise," poor Mr Brown stammered.

"I don't mean you." Lucy scrambled past him.

Where was the garden? She needed air. Only when the fresh wind brushed her heated cheeks, her heart returned to its normal pace. A sweet, enticing smell engulfed her. She stood in the middle of a picturesque flower garden, which Henry the gardener must have planted. Like an artist, she'd rhapsodised that day, so long ago.

What had he said about her smelling like wildflowers?

"Bah," Lucy uttered, startling the sparrows in the stone birdbath.

Marigolds, indeed.

CHAPTER 11

*L*ater, it occurred to Lucy that she'd missed the perfect opportunity to ask for her letter. She'd been so rattled when he discovered her under his desk, she'd completely forgotten all about it. She'd ask him at the next possible opportunity. However, the duke didn't make an appearance the entire afternoon and was absent even during supper. Lucy started to get edgy. How was she to accomplish her mission when he was so elusive?

After breakfast the next morning, Lucy slipped out of the dining room. She didn't feel like socialising with the house guests. She spent the remaining morning in the servant hall, where she talked to several footmen and housemaids, keeping them from their work. Their stories fascinated her. They scattered apart when Mrs Bates entered.

"I don't approve of servants conversing with guests, Miss." She pressed her lips in a disapproving line. Lucy suspected Mrs Bates had never really forgiven her for not telling her she was Lady Arabella's friend.

She smiled apologetically. "I know. It's your job not to approve."

"I believe the company is assembling in the blue salon to discuss the plans for the day." That was her way of saying it was time for Lucy to leave.

Lucy returned to the blue salon and listened to the women debate whether they should embroider, play another round of spillikins, or dare venture outside when it might rain again, soon. She suppressed a yawn.

"Miss Bell." An unassuming gentleman with spectacles stood in front of her. "Eugene Brown is my name." He bowed. "I'm the duke's secretary."

Lucy nodded. She'd nearly run him over, after she'd stormed out of the duke's study.

"The duke sent me to deliver this." He held out a small, blue, velvet pouch.

Lucy took it, puzzled. "What is it?"

"Marbles, Miss."

"Marbles!" She opened the pouch and spilled the contents onto her palm.

"The duke instructed me to deliver them to you personally. He said you'd know what to do with them."

"Yes! How inordinately thoughtful of him." Lucy said, surprised by this unpredictable man.

"If it isn't too forward of me to ask, Miss." He lowered his voice. "What are you going to do with them? One cannot help but be curious. It is rather out of the common to observe the duke dedicating an entire three hours searching for marbles."

"Oh, did he?" Lucy's eyes sparkled.

Mr Brown groaned. "He ransacked the entire study with singular determination. He refused any help. He eventually found them in the lowest drawer of his desk. Under a pile of documents."

"How marvellous! What do you think they were doing

there?" Lucy lowered her voice. "Do you think he secretly plays with marbles, Mr Brown?"

"If so, I have not yet caught him doing so."

"I need them for Jem."

Mr Brown nodded. "The lamp boy's little brother."

Lucy gave him an approving smile. "I'm impressed that you know who he is."

"The entire household knows who he is, Miss Bell. He, together with his brother Jimmy, ate every crumb of Mrs Springer's chicken pot pie."

"I hope they enjoyed every bite. That is rather nice of him, don't you think, that he is giving Jem his marbles? But it isn't just about Jem and Jimmy. I need to talk to him. It is proving to be rather difficult to get a hold of him in company here."

"He is a very busy man, Miss Bell."

"Mr Brown?" Lucy chewed on her lip.

"Yes, Miss Bell?"

"How does one talk to His Grace about business matters?"

"Business matters? Well. People usually make an appointment with me. And then, if it is important enough, they get invited to discuss the matter with His Grace."

"I see. Well, the matter I need to discuss with His Grace is of utmost importance. Therefore, Mr Brown, could you kindly make an appointment for me with His Highness—His Graceness—I mean, His Grace?"

"Certainly, Miss Bell. I will need my appointment book for this, however. His Graceness—I mean His Grace—is a very busy man, and his schedule is usually full." He furrowed his brow. "But I think I should be able to squeeze you in between the agricultural meeting and the water development meeting with the steward this afternoon. I shall let you know, Miss Bell."

"Mr Brown, you are gold."

He blushed.

Mr Brown did indeed squeeze her between the agricultural meeting and the water development meeting.

She sailed into the study, full of energy.

"Miss Bell! What now?" She saw the quick tensing of the duke's shoulders before his usual mask fell over his face.

"I have come to discuss some very important business matters," Lucy announced airily, to cover the somersaulting in her stomach. She stuck her nose in the air and sat down in the chair Mr Brown indicated.

"Do you need me to take notes, sir?" he enquired.

"Yes," Lucy said.

"No," Ashmore said simultaneously.

"This is a very important matter, so taking notes can't harm." Lucy rummaged about in her reticule and drew out a crumpled piece of paper covered in scribbles, which she set on the table, flattening it with her palm. "I've had to take some notes myself. So I don't forget anything, you see."

"I see." The duke leaned back in his chair and looked at Lucy with a glint in his eyes. "Well, Miss Bell. Reveal us the purpose of your, er, business visit. We're fairly agog with curiosity."

"Yes, and so you should be. It is a vexing affair." She frowned and turned the paper over, looking for the beginning of her notes. "Ah, here it is." She cleared her throat. "It's about Ophelia, you see."

The duke sighed. "No, I do not see. Nor does Mr Brown."

Mr Brown looked apologetic. "Who is this Ophelia, Miss Bell? I daresay you are not referring to the Shakespearean one?"

"How old are you, Your Grace?"

"And what does that have to do with anything?"

Lucy was irked by his cool, aloof manner.

"Approaching thirty-four, Miss Bell," Mr Brown responded. "And I am twenty-eight. In case that is relevant." He pushed up his spectacles.

"Thank you, Brown," Ashmore said. "Naturally, I would not know my own age. Now Miss Bell will no doubt enlighten us what my age has to do with this Ophelia."

"Thirty-four, really? Well. That is positively ancient. Anyway. I was just going to say that considering the fact you have lived in this house for thirty-four years, and Mr Brown, who has been in your employ for how long?"

"Nine years and three months, Miss Bell."

"Nine years and three months, and neither of you know Ophelia. That is really incredible."

Both men looked at her, flummoxed.

"Ophelia is the local midwife," she explained slowly, as if talking to a pair of dunces. "She was there the night you were born. Thirty-four years ago. It is understandable if you don't remember that incident. I also don't remember the night I was born. But what isn't so understandable is why that woman, who also was there the night your sister Arabella was born, and every other single member of the household born on these premises—to whom you owe the fact that you are now thriving and healthy—for I gather you are healthy, are you not?"

The duke choked, which Lucy took as a yes.

"So, given all this, it is quite a mystery why Ophelia would live alone and in poverty at the edge of Somersbrooke village. She's had to resort to begging. That isn't so under-standable to me. So, I thought you'd want to look into that matter. You might not be here today, healthy and thriving, if it hadn't been for Ophelia."

Mr Brown scribbled officiously.

"How did you come by this kind of information?" the duke asked.

"Oh." She shrugged. "I talk to people."

"With people you do not mean my house guests but—?"

"George the stable boy, Joseph the chimney sweep. Speaking of Joseph—"

He lifted a hand. "Brown, you will see to the matter."

"Yes, Your Grace."

"That was it, then?"

"Oh no, that's only the beginning. I have an entire list here. Let's see—"

"You will give the list to Brown."

"Yes. But there is one more thing that isn't on the list that is actually the primary reason I am here."

Both men looked at her.

She cleared her throat awkwardly. "It probably isn't a good idea that Mr Brown takes notes on this matter."

Mr Brown dropped the quill. "Would you like me to leave, Your Grace?"

"Stay. If it's a business matter, there is no reason Mr Brown shouldn't be present."

Lucy stirred uneasily in the chair. "Yes. It is a business matter. Of sorts. The thing is this." She wiped her clammy hands on her skirt. "I need you to write me a letter of recommendation, so Miss Hilversham takes me back. We've discussed this, if you recall. You said you'd write me that letter." An unwelcome blush stole into her cheek as she remembered that bantering conversation on the road, eternities ago. It had ended with her kissing him.

He steepled his hands and gave her a brooding stare. "I recall the conversation; however, I do not recall committing to writing that letter."

Lucy jumped up. "But you assured me you'd do so!"

"I did no such thing."

Lucy opened her mouth, then closed it with a snap. He was right. He'd never assured anything. He only said she might be agreeably surprised if the duke did write the letter. Which, of course, he'd never had any intention of doing. He'd misled her.

Lucy glowered at him. "That is positively beastly of you."

He remained unfazed. "I am no longer a patron of that institution. I believe that school to be a lost cause. I do not support lost causes."

Did he consider her a lost cause as well? The thought stung. "But you could be persuaded to change your mind about it if you attempted to be somewhat more open-minded?"

"Brown?"

Brown sat up straight. "Your Grace?"

"Do I ever allow myself to be persuaded to change my mind about anything?"

Brown didn't have to think. "No, Your Grace. Never."

Lucy clenched her hands, so her fingernails entered her palms. Who was that man who sat across from her, with that stony, implacable face? She did not know this stranger at all.

"There is another matter that I need to discuss with you." She placed her hands belligerently on her hips.

The duke repressed a sigh. "Yes, Miss Bell. We're waiting."

"It concerns your sister."

Ashmore frowned. "Arabella."

"Yes."

"And what does Arabella have to do with any of this? Pray enlighten me."

Lucy took a big breath. "You shouldn't marry her to Finbar. It's a colossal mistake."

He narrowed his eyes. "And why, Miss Bell, would that be a colossal mistake?"

Lucy rushed on. "Because they won't suit. Because, even

though he looks like Adonis, his character is too superficial. Because he isn't good enough for her. Because Arabella deserves better!" Lucy took another big breath and delivered her last punch. "Lastly, because she loves someone else."

They hadn't seen that coming. She let that piece of information sink in as she'd clearly taken the wind out of both men's sails.

"But she will marry Finbar just to please you. And be terribly unhappy for the rest of her life. You are her big brother, Henry, you should care about what she feels, and you should always see that your sister's happiness goes before the estate's or duty's or whatever it is you call it. You shouldn't bully her into marrying someone she doesn't love. And I know you care, even though you pretend you don't, or you want the rest of us to think you don't, for whatever mysterious reason that eludes me entirely, but no doubt is entirely clear to you. You are being pig-headed or a dunce, which I don't think you are, so it must be the pig-headedness. So there." She waved with one hand around after she finished the hopelessly mangled speech.

Mr Brown uttered a croak. He looked at Lucy in abject, fascinated horror. Not only had she called the duke by his first name, but she'd called him a dunce, and pig-headed. Twice. Then he looked at the duke, with an open mouth and wide eyes.

Ashmore kept staring at Lucy, and she kept staring back. They were back at the staring game, were they?

He got up and placed both hands on the desk and leaned forward. Lucy leaned forward as well. The air crackled. Every fibre in Lucy's body tingled.

Good God, he will do it, Lucy thought. *He will kiss me right in front of Mr Brown.*

He would have done it, too, if he hadn't recalled himself at the last moment.

"Let's get one thing clear once and for all," he said so quietly the hair on her arms stood on end. "My sister is my business, and my business alone. My sister's future is not up for discussion. You may trust that I consider Arabella's happiness of utmost importance. I'll thank you if in future you'll stop meddling with affairs that don't concern you."

"I take pig-headed back." Lucy turned to Brown. "It's a sad case of don't want to hear, don't want to see, don't want to speak." She placed both hands over her mouth, her ears, and her eyes. "Good day to you, gentlemen." She got up, nose in the air, and left the room rather grandly.

THE STUDY WAS SILENT. BROWN THREW A FURTIVE LOOK AT the duke.

"Brown."

"Your Grace?"

"What in the name of all that's good and holy am I to do?"

A look of understanding crossed Brown's face. He cleared his throat. "The truth?"

"If you please."

"I think you'd better marry her, Your Grace."

CHAPTER 12

*T*he next morning, the company slept in late. Lucy stood by the window of the drawing room, watching raindrops glide down the windowpane, when a low voice accosted her.

"Miss."

She turned. Felix Xaver Zornmann, the footman, stood in front of her. "Yes?"

"His Grace would have a word with you in the library. If you could follow me."

Lucy's stomach jolted. She followed him to the duke's wing.

He bowed and opened the library door for her.

Lucy swallowed.

She'd never been in the library before. It was a beautiful, oblong room, with windows on one side that allowed light to flood in, and tall, open bookshelves on the other. There was an ornate fireplace and several armchairs to invite reading and relaxation. The duke stood by the window, his back to the room, feet apart, his hands clasped behind his back.

Dressed in breeches, top boots and dark blue topcoat, he was a stern, commanding presence. Lucy wanted to flee. Instead, she positioned herself behind the green fauteuil.

Silence.

Either he wasn't aware that she was standing behind him, or he didn't give a tuppence and let her wait intentionally.

Should she clear her throat? Rustle about with her dress? Drop into a curtsy? Even before he opened his mouth to say something, he made Lucy feel foolish, awkward and entirely ill at ease.

On top of everything, her nose tickled.

Lucy grabbed the edge of the fauteuil for support and waited with a sense of doom for the inevitable. "Aaah-chooo!" Unfortunately, it wasn't a ladylike, cute kind of sneeze, but a violent eruption that sprayed moisture over the furniture. At least she'd got his attention. He spun around.

"Sorry." She covered her dripping nose with one hand. She never had a handkerchief when she needed one.

The duke produced one, and she blew her nose noisily, while he watched with a raised eyebrow. She crumpled it into a wet ball and held it out to him. He looked at it through his quizzing glass and flared his nostrils.

"You may keep the handkerchief, Miss Bell."

He couldn't have said that with more condescension.

"Thank you." Lucy sniffed. She had no place where to put it, so she kept pressing it into a smaller and smaller ball, while the duke kept looking at her in an austere way that gave her the chills.

What on earth was wrong with him? They were alone in the library. He could drop his mask.

"Well?" She raised her chin.

"Well?"

Lucy's nerves snapped. "If otherwise you have nothing to

say to me, I suppose I'll return to the drawing room." Wonderful, now she'd dismissed the duke in his own home. She turned and started marching to the door.

"Two things."

Lucy froze in her tracks.

"Well?" For heaven's sake. Couldn't she think of another word? "I mean, Your Grace." She kept forgetting that blasted title of his.

"First. Why are you here?"

Lucy gave him a blank look. "Because Felix asked me to come?"

"Felix?" He frowned. Then his brow cleared. "The footman. Pray, let us not repeat that discussion. I don't mean the library, but Ashmore Hall."

Was he stupid? She'd already told him the entire story when they'd met. She'd not retell it again. It was humiliating.

She lifted her chin and said in her most disdainful voice. "As I'm sure His Grace recalls, I mentioned the other day I'd like to ask His Grace for a letter of recommendation. Which His Grace has declined to write."

"I did not want to discuss this in Brown's presence. The letter of recommendation is superfluous."

"Why?"

"I shall explain momentarily. Regarding that letter, I do not believe one minute this is the genuine reason you are here. Do you care to explain yourself?"

"No." She lifted her chin mulishly.

"Did you run away from your previous position as a governess?"

She shrugged. "I didn't like it there, so I left."

He stared at her for a moment. "Forgive me, Miss Bell, but your entire story has neither hand nor foot. The only thing I know for a fact is you are the miss who nearly drowned my sister. Aside from involving her in a string of other misdeeds."

In other words, he didn't trust her. Lucy decided she hated him.

"I didn't purposefully attempt to drown her," she snapped, "as you very well know."

"Arabella is delighted you're here, and your presence seems to lift her spirits. She's been missing the company of her school friends."

"Of course. She's lonely here. You never have time for her."

His head jerked up as if her words hit home, but he quickly restrained himself. "If you don't care to reveal the true reason, you leave me no other choice but to believe that you intend to inveigle Arabella in some nonsense, least of which is to talk her out of the engagement she is to make at the end of the week."

So that was what bothered him. He feared her interference in their oh-so-orderly life.

The duke crossed his arms. "I don't know what ultimate reason you have for being here, but if it involves Arabella, if you jeopardise her engagement, or cause her to get into trouble or worse, I'll have no compunction to send you packing. Is this understood?"

"You're right. I intend to kidnap her and drag her to Gretna Green, where I'll force her to marry the local blacksmith. Really. Who do you think I am?" She jutted her chin.

For a moment he studied her intently. "I'm not sure. You are like a wind that refuses to be contained."

The silence between them was pregnant with unspoken words. Lucy held her breath.

"Secondly, Miss Bell." He gave her a veiled look. "It behoves me to discuss the inappropriate situation in which we found ourselves a few days back."

Lucy's head snapped up. Finally, he wanted to talk about why he paraded about as Henry.

"Neither of us could've helped it. Storm, force of nature and all that. You owe me an explanation. Are you going to tell me why you're leading a double life as a gardener?"

"No, I am not," he bit out. "Let me assure you, I didn't intend to deceive you. It was an unfortunate circumstance in which we both found ourselves through no choice of ours." He paced up and down.

"Good. So we agree."

"Be that as may, the situation was inappropriate, and you've been thoroughly compromised. Intentional or not, it is unforgivable to incriminate a lady's reputation, and it is my duty to rectify that." He stopped pacing and stood behind a chair. "Therefore—"

"But we've already thrashed this out if you recall. Nothing happened. No one knows. If you're apologising, it is quite gentlemanly of you to do so, though I can't for the life of me think of a reason why you ought to be responsible for the storm, or me jumping into the river to save the puppy, or the night at the shed—"

He closed his eyes, as if that memory pained him. Lucy felt a pang, because she cherished that memory.

"As I was saying—" he started.

"If we're to conclude you are not to blame, and neither am I, then there is nothing to be done about it. It was, as you say, just unfortunate. But it won't harm my reputation." Because she had none. She'd explained that, hadn't she?

"If you'd stop interrupting me, I could get to the point."

"Anyhow, how do you want to rectify this? Didn't you pay off the farmer?"

He drummed his fingers on the top rail of an armchair.

"Lucy. I am trying to propose marriage to you. If you'd stop interrupting me."

"What?" Lucy forgot to close her mouth.

"I intend to announce our engagement at the ball on Saturday." He stopped the thrumming and gripped the chair instead.

"But—now you've really lost your marbles. Everyone says you want to marry Lady Louisa because she is so perfect!"

"That was the plan. However, given what has happened, considering the circumstances, this is beside the point."

"But. Why?" She couldn't figure him out. One moment he threatened to send her packing, then he proposed marriage.

"As I have tried to explain, I am duty and honour-bound to rectify a highly incriminating situation that has compromised a lady of my sister's long-standing acquaintance." He couldn't have said that in a less pompous or stiff manner. Clearly, he didn't want to marry her in the least.

Lucy bristled. "But otherwise, I wouldn't be suitable, would I? I mean, Lady Louisa would be eminently suitable, wouldn't she? She has the breeding, the appearance, the lady-like behaviour, the language. She never falls into any rivers to rescue puppies, for one."

This was his cue to smile at the memory of that incident, but he kept up his forbidding look.

"No, Lady Louisa would never fall into any bodies of water. It is true you don't know how to behave in polite society. You are rash and you blurt out what you think, which is usually inappropriate given the situation. I never know what you'll do next. But this really is beside the point." Wrong reply. He was supposed to deny her claims, even out of politeness, not agree with her.

Lucy gritted her teeth. "Nonetheless, you are proposing marriage. In a rather cross, disagreeable kind of way. Because it's your obligation to fix a situation in which you have compromised a lady. Because it's your honour-bound duty."

He inclined his head at the word "duty".

"Had we met under normal circumstances, let's say, in a ballroom in London, you'd never have proposed to me. In fact, you'd never have even talked to me. At most, you'd have acknowledged me with a ducal nod from the distance because I'm Arabella's friend—the one who tried to drown her—so probably you'd have given me a marvellous cut to begin with."

There was a charged pause as he hesitated.

Lucy took a big breath and made a small curtsy. "I'm honoured by your dutiful but grumpy proposal, but I regret I must decline it. So now you can take a breath of relief and marry Lady Louisa, the perfect duchess."

He passed a hand over his eyes as if the discussion wearied him. "Do I really have to spell it out for you? Once the farmer's wife realises who I am, which she will, in due time, she'll not keep that delicious piece of information to herself. The Duke of Ashmore has spent an entire night in her shed – together with a girl, whom he introduced as his wife. This gossip will gallop faster than Wellington's hussars over the battlefield. Can't you see the scandal brewing? Before long, it'll explode in our faces. You really have no choice, Lucy."

"My name is Miss Bell. And you haven't been listening, Your Grace. I do have a choice. And my choice is not to marry you. In fact, I've just decided that you're the last person on earth I'd be induced to marry. Ever."

The duke remained unimpressed. "Four days. The ball is in four days. Get used to the idea. Then we will make the announcement."

She opened her mouth to tell him off, when he switched tactics. He stepped forward from behind the chair. There was a glint in his eyes.

"I don't understand why you're so upset at my proposal.

You yourself as much as propositioned marriage to me not so long ago. In addition," his voice turned silky, "to giving me a kiss." There was a minuscule curl in the left corner of his lips, so tiny that one needed a magnifying glass to see it, but it was there. "Your very first kiss, if I recall."

A hot blush spread over her entire body. If she could crawl under the Persian carpet to hide, she would. She covered her burning cheeks with her hands.

"It was a kiss for Henry the gardener and not for you. Besides, that was before I knew who you were. It doesn't count in the least, and I'll do my best to forget it ever happened. You deceived me. You lied to me. You're being ungentlemanly and o-odious to remind me of this."

"Very odious of me, indeed." He clearly enjoyed himself. "The kiss didn't count, hm?" He stood right in front of her.

"Oh! You! I am. Very. Very. Very. Angry." She tipped her forefinger against his waistcoat to emphasise the 'very'.

He caught her hand in his in a crushing grip and pulled her towards him. "Stop fighting, Lucy," he murmured.

His eyes shone with a disturbing light. The beehive in her stomach began buzzing again. Her mouth dried. She forgot to breathe. If he held her even closer, and lowered his head, precisely as he was doing right now, she'd think he was just Henry and do the unthinkable by kissing him again.

That wasn't to be borne.

Lucy struggled and freed herself. He dropped his hands.

"We will make the announcement at the ball."

"Bah." Thoroughly rattled, Lucy whirled around and intended to underscore her point with the satisfying slamming of the door. Alas, she was denied this gratification. Felix must have heard her stomping approach, for the door opened magically to let her through.

Throwing Ashmore a last thunderous scowl, Lucy turned to see him do something utterly shocking.

He grinned.

Lucy stumbled. With a kitten-like mewl, she whirled out of the library.

CHAPTER 13

*L*ucy threw two dresses, a shawl and her reticule into her carpetbag. Arabella would have to forgive her for taking the dresses. She had several coins left, enough for the stagecoach to Bath. She would beg on her knees for Miss Hilversham to take her in. Without the duke's letter.

Lucy slipped out through the servants' entrance. No one saw her leave. She hurried through the forest to the main road. It would be a long walk. She needed to arrive at the inn before the night set and someone noticed she'd left.

Marriage!

Lucy laughed harshly.

The irony of it all. Arabella's silly coins in the wishing well had almost done the trick.

Lucy increased her speed. The carpetbag pressed on her shoulder like a load of stones. Her heart felt heavier and heavier… until tears fell.

She wiped them away angrily. *For heaven's sake, he's a duke. He's a duke. He's a duke.* That was the rhythm she chanted to herself, but her brain refused to believe it.

He's Henry, he's Henry, he's Henry, her heart replied.

She turned around and saw Ashmore Hall between the trees. The sandstone glinted orange in the light of the setting sun. How grand it looked, how proud. How impossible it all was.

She walked backwards, unable to tear her gaze away from the building.

Then she fell. The bag hurtled out of her hand and she somersaulted several times down a seemingly endless hole. Not having paid attention to where she was going, she'd strayed off the path and fallen down a deep ditch.

The muddy walls were steep and vertical, and the bottom filled with ankle-deep water from the recent storm.

Lucy groaned.

She'd covered her head with her arms, so she didn't sustain any injury, aside from a few scrapes and bruises.

She was caked with mud. Her bag soaked in the quaggy water.

Lucy tried to climb up the steep walls, but the earth crumbled beneath her fingers and she slid back again to the bottom.

It was getting dark. There was only one thing left to do. Lucy took a big breath.

"Heeeelp!"

There was silence. Even the birds had stopped chirping.

The silence, the steep, earthy walls, the descending darkness enveloped her, pressed down on her, choked her off her breath. It was too tight, too narrow, too dark. There was no space, they would not hear her cries. She was a little girl again, back in the cold, grim pit.

Mama couldn't hear her. Maybe if she cried longer and louder.

Icy fingers crawled over her clammy skin, like tentacles spreading over her body, her neck, her face, digging deep into her erratically hammering heart, as if to squeeze out its life force.

Lucy gasped for air. Her throat emitted raspy sounds. She was so terrified she couldn't even scream.

Wet earth everywhere. Darkness.

Cold. Hunger.

Mama.

Pressing her eyes shut, she rolled herself up into a ball, rocked back and forth and whimpered.

"Lucy! Where are you?"

"Where are you?"

"It came from down there. God's teeth! There's a little girl in the open grave. And she's alive."

"Pull her out, Jerry, pull her out. There, there, little girl. Joris and Jerry will help you out."

"Be careful. Maybe she's a spectre, or an undead one come alive to eat our souls."

"That's a horrid bag of moonshine. Can't you see the coffin's right down there? 'Tis old Jeremy in the box. Bit the dust on account of a barrel fever. Why didn't they close the hole? She must've fallen in. What's a little one like her doin' all alone in a graveyard? She can't be older than two. There, there, little one. We'll get you out. She's got blue lips. God knows how long she's been down there."

"How pretty she is. Her dress is very fine. Can we keep her?"

"I don't know, Joris. Someone's bound to look for her."

"But if she ain't belongin' to no one?"

"Maybe. Then we might as well keep her."

A familiar voice penetrated through her fog of terror. But she must've imagined it, because she stopped hearing the voice.

Maybe she'd fainted. Maybe she'd fallen asleep. The voice sounded again, closer.

"Lucy!" The voice was right above her.

She jerked.

"Look at me, Lucy."

She kept her eyes clenched shut and shook her head.

The voice swore in a familiar Henry-manner. "I can't go down there, Lucy. The only way to get you out is if you open your eyes and do exactly as I say."

"Henry?"

"Yes. Can you open your eyes and look up? I'm right above you. I don't like looking down. By Jove. I will end up down the ditch next to you if I keep looking down."

Lucy opened her eyes wide. "Are you afraid of heights?"

There was a pause. Then a muffled reply.

"I didn't understand."

"I said: yes. Blast it." An irritated oath followed. "Don't go anywhere. I'll be back soon."

"As if I could," Lucy muttered. She wrapped her arms around her and waited.

After ten minutes, he returned. "Careful now."

A rope dangled right next to her.

"Take the rope in both hands. Do you have it?"

"Yes."

"Now stem both your feet against the mud wall."

"It doesn't work. The earth is too soft."

"Try again."

Lucy planted both feet against the mud wall, but it kept crumbling.

"You can do this. I know you can. A girl who can jump from a bridge straight into a brook to save a three-legged puppy can also climb up a blasted mud wall. Don't disappoint me."

Lucy choked back a laugh. Then her foot found a tighter patch of packed mud towards the right. She tested it with her foot, pressed against it. It held.

"Good girl. Now the other foot and heave yourself up." She gingerly placed the second foot above it and pulled herself up on the rope.

She climbed up, step by step, until she reached him. His face peered cautiously over the edge as he pulled on the rope.

"You're almost there."

A hand gripped her arm and lifted her.

"Hold on tight." She felt herself lifted, and she clung to the shoulders and arms that held her. Then she was out of the hellish ditch.

"Does anything hurt?"

Lucy shook her head. "I'm only muddy." Her teeth clattered. "And cold."

He pulled off his gardener's jacket and put it around her shoulders. Then he lifted her onto his horse, which was tethered to a tree nearby. He climbed up behind her and rode back to the house.

Lucy curled against his jacket and inhaled the scent of tobacco and leather. She felt his warmth, his heartbeat.

"How did you find me?"

"One of the workers clearing the trees saw you disappear in the forest. I was working in the garden when he told me he thought it was odd that one of the houseguests would scramble off into the wild part of the forest where the ditches are. I knew it had to be you." He swore. "Why didn't you answer when I called you? I only heard a vague 'help' and then nothing. I feared the worst." His voice was harsh.

"I—hate being enclosed. It makes me panic and then I'm incapable of functioning."

"You could've spent the night out there all alone." He clenched his jaw. "What an utterly hare-brained thing to do, running off like that."

"I suppose it was stupid of me." Lucy crumpled under his scathing scrutiny. "I didn't think."

"You rarely think before you act, do you?"

"Only when someone bullies me into doing something I don't want to do," she muttered.

"Is this what you think? That I bully you?"

"Absolutely. Yes. Sometimes. Not on purpose. Oh, I don't know!" Why was he looking at her as though he cared? It made her feel all hot and muddled inside. "The truth is, I don't know what to think anymore. You can seem awfully cross and unforgiving and horridly proud when you are the duke. It's rather intimidating and makes me feel like I'm inadequate and then I just want to run."

There was a taut silence.

"Oh dear. I shouldn't have said that."

"It's unfortunate I have this effect on you," he said after a heartbeat. "I apologise if my disposition makes you feel inadequate. It's not intentional. I suppose it is—" he seemed to struggle with himself. "It's how I am. Spontaneity and a lighter outlook on life, like you and Arabella have, is something I never possessed."

"I didn't mean to say that you are wrong in having a more reserved disposition. Can you imagine a world of only Arabellas and Lucies? That would be fairly awful. It's just—I prefer when you're being Henry, that's all. Just a little more."

He sighed. "Once in a while I like to put on simpler clothes and work in the gardens. It helps me think. When things get—too much—sometimes, I even like to take the cart and drive about the countryside and pick up plants. That's all there is to it, Lucy. You've patched yourself up an image of a man who doesn't exist."

Lucy felt a lump in her throat. "I don't think I imagined it."

He looked at her with a thoughtful frown. "Am I being forgiven for my cross and bullying behaviour?"

Lucy nodded. "I still won't marry you," she said gruffly into his jacket as she clung to him.

"You've made your sentiments more than clear. For your peace of mind, I won't pressure you into anything—for the time being. However, we're not done with this topic. For now, I insist that you stay here for Arabella's pleasure—and as my guest. If you please."

"Would it really please you?"

"It would."

"Well then, I'll stay." She beamed at him through the muck that caked her face.

"You're full of contradictions," he grumbled. He looked at her as if she posed an unsolvable riddle.

"You've mud on your cheeks," she said breathlessly.

"So do you." He wiped it off gently with one hand and tugged an errant curl behind her ear. His finger lightly brushed her jaw.

It took him awfully long to lift her off his horse and set her down, and even then, his hands lingered at her waist. He carried her into the house, all the way to her room, calling for servants on the way.

She was given a hot bath, a warm meal, tucked into bed with three blankets and warm bricks tucked by her feet. Lucy had never had such a fuss made over her.

She fell asleep feeling that maybe she and the duke had finally found some truce.

She dreamed that there was a marble statue of the duke standing in the corridor. She chipped away at it with a hammer and chisel, and underneath appeared flesh.

"There you are, Henry," she cried in relief and threw her arms around him. "I thought you'd disappeared."

"I've been there all the time." He smiled his old Henry smile. He held out his hand to her.

Then she remembered why she couldn't take his hand.

The fall into the ditch had brought it all back again.

Lucy shook her head and silent tears rolled down her face. She could never take his hand because of who she was.

CHAPTER 14

*T*he next day, the weather still hadn't improved, and the company stayed inside. Following Mr Fridolin's example, Lucy went to the library. The duke's collection of books was impressive, containing everything from musical scores to first folios of Shakespearean plays. She spent most of the afternoon browsing through the books, with no other sound in the library than the occasional flipping of paper.

After an uneventful supper, the ladies went to the drawing room while the men drank port and smoked cigars in the billiard room.

Miss Emma Stilton suppressed a yawn. "I hope the men join us soon. It's so boring without them."

"I daresay they have to have a smoke first." Lady Conway fanned herself with a peacock fan.

"Dreadful vice, smoking." Lady Rawleigh shuddered. "I don't know what they see in it."

Lady Conway agreed. "Conway told me he quit a long time ago, but I can tell he didn't. His clothes reek of cigar smoke every evening. It would never occur to me to say anything, however."

"How fortunate Ashmore doesn't smoke." Lady Louisa produced a sewing frame and made dainty stitches. "It is so very vulgar. I wouldn't be able to bear it."

Interesting, Lucy thought. She could disillusion Lady Louisa; however, decided against it. Let her discover in her own time that she had the duke all wrong. Lucy pulled out a book and read in the armchair, ignoring the women.

"Must we talk about smoking? It is such an unrefined topic. Let us talk about something else." Lady Rawleigh curled her lips.

"Pray, what are you reading, Miss Bell?" Miss Jane looked at Lucy's book with curiosity.

"*The Mysteries of Udolpho*." She'd picked up the book earlier in the library. "I enjoy Ann Radcliffe's stories of terror and the supernatural."

"Oh no, such tales frighten me. I wouldn't like to read anything of the kind here. I heard there are ghosts in Ashmore Hall." Miss Stilton looked worried.

"Oh, every grand house has their house ghosts. We have several." Arabella replied cheerfully. "We have a white lady who walks on the roof shortly before an unfortunate event is to happen." Arabella pretended to be unaware of the terror she instilled in the younger ladies.

The ladies gasped.

"That doesn't frighten me as much as the graveyard at midnight," Lucy put in, remembering an incident in which they'd snuck out at night from the Seminary to visit the graveyard.

Arabella grinned at the memory.

Jane shuddered. "Yes, but draughty galleries at midnight are also frightful. Particularly when the eyes of portraits are upon you."

"Yes. Especially since you might run into the moaning man there." Lucy shivered dramatically and wrapped her arms around herself.

"The moaning man." Emma clung to her sister. "Who is that?"

"Isn't he the one who got half-beheaded, Arabella?" Lucy flipped a page in her book.

"No, he's the cook who got walled up in the Southern wall. Half-headed Joe walks in the East wing."

Both Stilton sisters turned pale.

Emma wailed, "How positively frightful! Isn't our room in the East wing? I shan't be able to sleep at night."

"I don't believe in ghosts. They are a manifestation of a befuddled mind," announced Lady Louisa. "Reading books like Miss Radcliffe's excites your senses and causes you to hallucinate."

"Why, Lady Louisa, wherever do you get those notions?" Lucy peeped up from her book with an imp lurking in her eyes.

Unaware that Lucy intentionally egged her on, Lady Louisa went on. "It is commonly known that reading excitable stories does not improve the mind."

"Quite so." Lady Bleckingham nodded.

Arabella looked at Lady Louisa curiously. "Are you never frightened at night?"

"I have an intrepid mind and a balanced constitution. I know no fear." She sniffed.

Lucy's and Arabella's eyes met. Lucy's brimmed with mischief, and Arabella laughed, turning it into a cough.

The white woman would walk on the roof of Ashmore Hall tonight.

From having listened to Lady Louisa's chatter the entire afternoon, Lucy knew she suffered from insomnia and didn't retire to bed until after midnight. To make sure Louisa was awake, Arabella would knock on her door under a pretense.

"I'll say I can't sleep and that I came to pick up my volume on Shakespeare's sonnets that I lent her earlier. Not that she reads it; we both know she doesn't read. I'm certain she only asked to borrow it because Ash stood nearby and said he liked Shakespeare."

Ashmore Hall was built in an E-shape with three wings, with Lady Louisa's room conveniently placed at the tip of the first leg of the E, her windows facing the front and the middle court. If Lucy walked on the roof of the middle wing, Louisa could see her, if she went to the window facing the inner court.

"You'll have to get her to look out of the window just at midnight." Lucy said as she powdered her face white.

Arabella nodded. "I'll think of something. I'll try to get her to open the window. I can't wait to see her face. Oh, Lucy, I haven't had this much fun since we left the Seminary." She returned to her room to wait for her cue.

Shortly before midnight, Meg scratched on Lucy's door. They'd told her about the plan and she'd show Lucy the way up to the roof.

Meg almost dropped the lamp. "Oh Miss, you look terrifying!"

Lucy had painted dark circles around her eyes. With a long, white gown and her tangled hair flowing open down her back, she frightened even herself.

"Hush, Meg, no one's to see me. Let's go."

They darted to the servants' quarters, up the narrow, winding stairs. At the end of the corridor, they entered a cluttered little tower room filled with stacked old chairs and tables.

Meg opened a small window that led out to the roof. "You can get out here, Miss. But be careful!"

Lucy climbed out of the window and stood on a flat foot-wide platform leading to the chimneys. Cool night air blew into her face. The full moon and twinkling stars lit up the sky. It couldn't get any better. They'd see a white figure from the distance, but not who it was. A low parapet at the edge would prevent her from toppling off. Having reached the chimney, she walked to the end of the wing and back.

Her long hair streamed in the wind, and she hoped that her face was sufficiently pale. A feeling of freedom rushed through her. She lifted her arms and pretended to float.

"Behold, the white lady walks." This was even more fun than when she pretended to be a ghost back at the Seminary in Bath.

A shrill shriek pierced through the night.

Lady Louisa. Lucy grinned. So much for an intrepid mind and balanced constitution. Lucy nearly laughed as she imagined Louisa fainting with fright. Satisfied that her mission was accomplished, she lingered for a moment longer, lifted her ghostly face up, allowing the moonlight to shine on it, then turned slowly, and drifted to the tower room, where Meg waited for her. Throwing a look back over her shoulder, Lucy froze. There was a tall, male figure standing in the window of the opposite wing, watching her.

Something quivered in her stomach.

"Botheration," Lucy muttered.

For on that other side were the duke's apartments.

CHAPTER 15

Someone knocked on the door. Lucy expected Arabella, and was surprised to see Mrs Bates.

"Miss Bell. The duke requests you to come down to the blue salon." The housekeeper gave her a meaningful look.

"Now?"

"Immediately."

"It's past midnight."

"I know."

"Why?"

"I wouldn't know, Miss. He's expecting you." She looked at Lucy's face. "May I suggest washing your face first?"

Should she pretend she'd been sleeping and had no idea what had happened? But no. That seemed cowardly. Lucy scrubbed the paint off her face and followed Mrs Bates down to the drawing room.

She arrived at the same time as the duke. Her mouth fell open at his dishevelled appearance.

His hair was rumpled, and his shirt hung out of his trousers as if he'd either dressed quickly, or was interrupted in getting undressed.

"Miss Bell. A word with you," Henry ground out. He held the door to the drawing room open. He didn't even close the door when he exploded. "What in everything that's good and holy were you thinking?"

Lucy looked sheepish. "I'm sorry. It was an old prank from our school days. I suppose it's not what ladies do." She was in her nightgown and her bare toes peeked out from under the hem. She felt at a disadvantage.

"What ladies do?" He looked at her as if she had three heads. "You scrambled around on top of Ashmore Hall! You could have fallen!"

"Oh no. I was not in any danger. The parapet up there would've prevented me from falling off."

"The parapet hasn't been maintained for years. You should've never been out there to begin with."

"I couldn't resist having some fun." Lucy knew that sounded childish.

"Fun?" He raised his voice.

"Yes, fun. A word you, Your Grace, seem to be entirely unacquainted with." She felt her hackles raise.

"You could've fallen and broken your neck! How, in any way, is that fun?" he roared.

"I wouldn't have fallen," she shouted back. "I told you it was entirely safe!"

"You're irresponsible, rash and act without thinking of the consequences of your actions. You fall into ditches and insist upon filling my house with all sorts of animals. And now you climb around on my roof and put your life in danger—and you tell me it's fun. It's intolerable!"

"And you! What about you?" Lucy stomped with her naked foot on the carpet, which didn't make any impression at all. "You're a liar, impostor and an arrogant oaf! You pretend to be someone you are not, thinking you're better than everyone else because you have oh so nobly sacrificed all your dreams and desires for that artificial role of duty and honour you insist on playing. Yet it bores you to tears. You bore yourself to tears! And you're determined to despise everyone else and look down on them! At least most people here are honest with their stuffiness and artificiality."

She stuck out a finger and wagged it under his nose. "You're a hypocrite! So don't go about despising others if they're having a speck of fun in this dreary life." She stomped her foot on the carpet again. "And, for heaven's sake, stop pretending to be so insufferably bored with everything!"

A horrified gasp came from the door. When they turned around, they saw a group of shell-shocked ladies, clad in nightgowns and shawls, watching in open-mouthed astonishment as Lucy and Henry ripped into each other. They must have heard every word. Lady Louisa covered her mouth. Arabella's eyes were saucers and her hands flew to her chest. The Stilton girls looked like they were about to faint.

"Interesting." There was a gleam in the Dowager Duchess' eyes. "If you two have finished slaughtering each other in public, may I suggest we proceed to having some tea? I believe we could all do with a midnight snack, now that we've discovered the ghost of Ashmore Hall is not a ghost at all."

"Oh, dear." Lucy looked around for a mouse hole.

A deep, red flushed crept up Henry's throat. He lifted a hand and rubbed his neck. It was as if only now he'd realised his surroundings.

"I seem to have forgotten myself," he said into the shocked silence. Turning to Lucy, he said, "Pray accept my apologies for having raised my voice, Miss Bell, even though the occasion warranted it. It was ungentlemanly of me."

"See!" she hissed. "There you go again." She whirled out of the room.

"What did I say now?" he addressed no one in particular, frustrated. For one moment it looked like he was about to rush after her. Then he remembered his audience.

"You never told me you two seem to know each other—from somewhere." Arabella frowned.

"As I mentioned, this is entirely a mistake on my side. If you will excuse me." He bowed stiffly to the ladies and fled.

"But, I don't understand." Louisa looked after his retreating figure. "What did she mean with Ashmore pretending to be someone he is not?"

"I've never seen him so angry before. In fact, I didn't know the Duke of Ashmore was capable of getting angry at all," mused Jane.

"If I hadn't seen it with my own eyes, I wouldn't have believed it. Come on, Jane, let's return to bed." Lady Bleckingham pulled her daughter away.

"But—but," Louisa gasped for air like a fish. "She called him an arrogant o-oaf!"

"Shocking." The dowager cleaned her spectacles on her shawl.

"Indeed! Such an excess of emotion is unbecoming for a lady. How can such appalling behaviour be tolerated?"

Arabella groped for an answer. The dowager answered in her stead.

"You must be right, Lady Louisa. In medieval times, people used to be thrown into the dungeons every time they criticised their betters. No doubt you would prefer we reintroduce such customs. Now, if we may proceed to the tea tray, I'm fairly starved, even if it is…"—she flicked her pocket watch open— "long past midnight."

CHAPTER 16

"*L*ucy, how could you say all those things! In my entire life, I've never heard him shout in such a manner." Arabella had followed Lucy to her room.

"I said terrible things. My infernal mouth! I suppose he's right and the entire idea was stupid and childish to begin with." Lucy's shoulders slumped. "I just couldn't resist Lady Louisa. Teach her a lesson. I'll have to apologise to him, will I not?"

"Honestly, I've never seen him so angry before. Why didn't you tell me you knew Ash from somewhere? The way you talked, or rather, shouted presupposes a degree of familiarity that only people of greater intimacy have."

"Because we—he—I didn't—I mean—" Lucy sighed. "It's really not in the way you think."

"But you've met before."

"Yes."

"In London? At the season?"

"No. Look, Arabella—"

"I'm disappointed. I thought we were friends and told each other everything."

"It's not like that. I mean, I didn't know who he was when I met him. I thought he was someone else then."

"Oh! Tell me!"

Lucy hesitated. Tell her she'd met him when he was a gardener? That she'd lost her heart to someone who didn't exist? That the very thought of him made her heart race? But that she didn't care a tuppence for the duke? That she fairly detested him? How muddled was that? How could she explain to Arabella what she didn't understand herself? Lucy placed her hands against her burning cheeks and shook her head.

"I can't. Really, I can't."

Arabella sent her a long, pained look.

"There was a time when we had no secrets between us. I wish you could trust me more."

She left the room.

Lucy stared after her. Oh dear, what a muddle. She was not only bitterly at odds with the brother, now she'd also hurt her friend.

Lucy tossed and turned in bed, sleep eluding her. Would the duke throw her out, now? She'd proven him right. She wasn't a good person to have around. She'd set the entire household on its head, antagonised and terrified the guests, and called him names. Good heavens. The letter! She slapped her forehead. Strange how she'd forgotten all about it. He'll never write her that dratted letter now. He'll throw her out instead. She wouldn't wait for that to happen. She'll go quietly, first thing in the morning.

Lucy climbed out of bed and drew the curtains aside to let the moonlight flood through the windows. She froze. Outside, on the roof, there was a figure. A lone person leaning against the roof, looking up at the sky.

Without thinking twice, Lucy left her room, ran up the stairs to the tower room and climbed out.

She walked along the narrow edge, holding onto the parapet, and stopped next to him.

"I thought you were afraid of heights."

"I am. That is why I'm looking at the sky, not on the ground." He gripped the chimney edge so tightly his knuckles were white.

She looked up at the sky. It was a clear night, and the stars twinkled brightly.

"This is Ursa mayor, the great bear." Henry pointed. He wore a shirt, and his sleeves were rolled up.

"No, it's not," Lucy replied. "It's Orion the hunter."

"There is Polaris the North star, right there." He pointed again. "On line with the two other stars. That means that Ursa is there."

"That's Betelgeuse. It's part of Orion. Polaris is there." Lucy pointed to the sky.

"You have it all mixed up."

"They taught us well in the Seminary. I know my stars when I see them," Lucy insisted.

"So do I. We used to spend many nights sleeping under the starry night. David and I." There was a weighty silence between them. "This is where he died."

Lucy looked at him in horror. "We used to come out here. This very spot. Except back then there was no parapet."

Lucy covered her mouth with her hands.

"He fell." He stared at his hands, motionless. "I could not hold on to him."

Lucy's breath came out gasping. "I—didn't know. I am so sorry. So truly sorry, from the bottom of my heart." She wrung her hands. "I wouldn't have done that childish prank had I known. Really, I wouldn't."

Henry sighed.

Lucy dropped her head and turned to go. "I'll leave first thing tomorrow. You were right about me all the time. I'm no good for Arabella. Or your guests here. Or, or you. I can't seem to help getting everyone who knows me in trouble. But this—" She shook her head. "This is unforgivable."

He reached out and took her hand. "I want you to stay."

Her hand twitched in his big one. "You can't really want that," she said thickly.

"I want you to stay." His voice was low, insistent.

Lucy puzzled over what exactly he meant. Stay up here with him on the roof? Or stay at Ashmore Hall? As a guest? As something more? Her heart squeezed at the thought of leaving this place. Leaving him.

They stood in silence, the night air brushed gently over their faces.

Lucy peeped at him. He had his eyes closed, as if thinking intently. "Will you tell me what happened?" She whispered.

At first, he didn't reply. "This used to be our favourite place for playing. We used to lie on the roof like this. Hiding from our tutors. They never guessed we were up here. How reckless we were. Back then, there was nothing to prevent you from falling. David slipped. I still don't know how that happened. Whether he fell over a brick or tripped over his own feet. I used to wonder over it endlessly, Lucy. Whether there was something I could've done to prevent it."

Lucy gripped his hand tighter. "It was an accident. It wasn't your fault," she whispered.

"It was. It was my duty to take care of him. I was his elder brother. I failed him and it cost his life. I never should've let him come out here. He hung onto the edge for a while. I tried to help him up. He held my hand. But then —" his voice broke, but after a moment he pulled himself together with an iron will, "but then he slipped through my hand." His voice was bleak. "He was only fourteen. My mother died soon afterwards, giving birth to Arabella. The grief had weakened her. A year later my father died. He completely let himself go. I'm responsible for wiping out half of my family."

Lucy lifted his hand against her wet cheek. "No. You're too harsh with yourself. None of it was your fault. You were a child."

"My childhood ended that day."

Now she understood. Why he was so overprotective towards Arabella. His fierce sense of duty and honour. The marble mask he wore. Why it was difficult for him to just be himself.

"So that's why you became the consummate duke." Lucy felt a leaden sadness weigh her down. "Then the role squashes you so, you have to escape from it, in small increments of freedom—as Henry the gardener. But you always return to retreat behind your dukely mask. It's your duty. Duty or death. If you don't fulfil your duty, it costs other people's lives."

His hand jerked in hers. "Duty or death." He laughed harshly. "How melodramatic. But it's more or less true. After David and Mother died, my father cast aside his role and the duty that came with it. And look what happened: he killed himself in the process."

"What happened?"

"My father never wanted to be a duke. Like me. That's the only thing we shared. He'd always led a fast life. My mother turned a blind eye to it all. The gambling. The Drury Lane doxies. After she died, he just got worse. He gambled and spent his time in the taverns, getting drunk. And actresses." His lip curled.

"Harriet Westington." Lucy threw him a sideways glance. The legendary actress of Drury Lane.

"Harriet Westington. A bigger strumpet never lived. He

nearly ruined himself over her. She's entirely corrupted, and that is no doubt because of her profession."

Lucy fidgeted. "You can't throw them all into one pot, Henry. Not all actresses are like her."

"I daresay the majority are. Thanks to her, I have no great love for that breed of people. They're a lying, cheating lot."

Lucy swallowed. "What happened?"

"One night, on the way back from the village, he fell off his horse and broke his neck. He was too drunk to stay on top of it."

"And then you became duke." Lucy's heart ached for the boy he must've once been.

"Shortly before he died, he'd sold a small portion of our land that wasn't entailed to maintain that woman. To Tilbury."

"Lady Louisa's father."

"Yes. In practical terms, it's a negligible chunk of land. But it includes a part of the forest where, as a child, I liked to play —with David."

"Of course you'd want it back," Lucy said softly.

"Not only because of that. It should have gone to Arabella. It's my duty to fix my father's mistakes."

"By marrying Lady Louisa." Lucy guessed that Tilbury must be offering the land as part of her dowry.

He was silent. He didn't have to say aloud that that had been the original plan. Until Lucy came along and turned everything upside-down.

She swallowed. "That's why you are cross with me. You'd rather marry Louisa because of the land."

"We've discussed this. The fact is neither of us have a choice. You and I have to get married."

"You always say this, and it's infuriating."

"It would solve your problem. You'd have a home and

wouldn't have to spend the rest of your life at the Seminary leading a lowly life as a teacher."

"You offer marriage without love. I find that even more lowly."

"Love?" He laughed harshly. "My father believed in love. Look where that led him. To near ruination. He nearly dragged the rest of us down with him. I've spent my entire life rebuilding what my father nearly ruined. I won't make the same mistake."

Lucy shivered. She pulled her hand away. "What about Lady Louisa and the land?"

"I'll get it back another way." He sounded hard.

She shook her head. "You'll blame me for the rest of your life. I don't want to be responsible for you not getting it because of me."

"No need to worry. I usually get what I want."

"You are so—so—" Lucy spluttered.

He raised an eyebrow.

"Arrogant."

"Very well, Lucy. If it makes you feel better. We will not announce the engagement tomorrow at the ball. We'll take it slowly and wait until the guests have left."

"Do I have any choice in the matter?"

"No."

Lucy huffed and returned to the window. Before she climbed back, she saw him gazing at the sky, tall, pensive and utterly lonely.

CHAPTER 17

$\mathcal{T}$he ladies greeted Lucy with chill politeness at breakfast. The gentlemen were out on an early morning deer hunt. Lucy wished she could have joined them, even though she detested hunting. No one mentioned the previous night's fiasco, yet everyone gave her the cold shoulder. Lady Louisa didn't even nod to her. Arabella sat straight and stiff in her chair and had not met Lucy's eyes when she entered.

Lucy took a big breath, walked up to Lady Louisa, who lifted her teacup to her lips. "I apologise for frightening you last night. It was a silly schoolgirl's trick. Badly done. I hope no harm has come of it."

Lady Louisa set down her cup carefully. "Miss Bell. I am surprised you are still here. Didn't Ashmore ask you to leave?"

Lucy crumpled the napkin between her fingers.

Arabella's voice was haughty and cold. "Miss Bell is my guest. Ash has no right to ask my guests to leave without my permission. And I never throw out my guests, no matter what they do."

Lucy looked at her friend, surprised, but grateful that she defended her. She bit into a slice of toast. It tasted like a mouthful of dry ash.

"What's the plan for today?" she asked Arabella with forced cheerfulness.

"I'll accompany Lady Louisa on a walk to the Abbey after breakfast." Arabella didn't meet her eyes. That Lucy wasn't welcome to join was left unspoken.

Lucy nodded woodenly.

A footman entered and approached Lucy. "The dowager duchess would like to see you, miss."

Glad to have an excuse to leave the dining room, Lucy set down her napkin and went to the dowager's drawing room.

"Sit down, sit down." The dowager pointed to an ottoman across from her. She studied Lucy with a pierced look.

"Show me your teeth."

"Why?"

"Oblige me." She grabbed her chin to look at her teeth. Lucy tried to pull away, but she tightened her grip.

"I cleaned them with tooth powder, if that is what you want to know."

The dowager dropped her gnarled hand. "Hump. You have crooked teeth." Her shrewd eyes looked over her figure critically. "Your figure is too small and your hips are too narrow. But that's no reason for not being able to carry babies."

"I'm not a horse, Your Grace," Lucy replied, stung.

"If they were to choose duchesses like horses, we'd all be saved a considerable heap of trouble. Horses breed well and reliably, if one chooses them wisely."

"I don't understand."

"I may be deaf at times, but I'm not blind. Regardless of how improbable it may seem, you seem to have caught my grandson's attention."

138

"I did. He dislikes me excessively." She was certain that the duke did. But the gardener? She felt a tingling in her chest.

"I'm not so sure about that."

Something jolted through Lucy. "Why?"

"Why? Because we witnessed a lover's quarrel in the middle of the night."

A bright flush covered Lucy's cheeks. "It's not like that at all, Your Grace."

"Ah, it is not? Then what is it? Pray enlighten me."

"It is just—I suppose we don't get along, that's all." She experienced a gamut of perplexing emotions. *Lover's quarrel.* Was it really true? Was that what she felt towards Henry? Was that what he could feel towards her? Unthinkable.

Her heart started to hammer painfully.

"That is the understatement of the century. You seem to be able to draw a side out of Henry that he shows to no one else. He's not usually prone to temper tantrums and most certainly not to lover's quarrels. Nonetheless, I witnessed both yesterday. Has he proposed?" Lucy kneaded her hands in her skirt as she attempted to stutter a response. "I see he has." The older woman tapped her cane against the floor impatiently. "You'd better marry him."

Lucy jumped up. "Oh no, no no. I never meant—this is terrible!" She paced the floor, then plopped down on the ottoman again and wrung her hands. "Yes, he proposed, but he didn't mean it. He was excessively cross about it. I'm certain the last thing he wants to do is marry me."

"My girl. Let's get one thing straight. No Ashmore ever does something he—or she—does not want to do. It is a law of life. Now. If Ashmore proposed, he wants to marry you."

Lucy backed away. "I'd make a terrible duchess!"

"I entirely agree. You're like a hurricane within this house

139

and estate. You create minor disasters wherever you go. You're entirely unsuitable to be a duchess." She sniffed.

"Well then, we're in agreement." Lucy clutched at her dress.

"Yet maybe that's precisely what Henry needs," the dowager went on. "Little disasters daily to jolt him out of his shell. Little reminders that life is unpredictable and messy. Not this milk and water miss that is better kept in a porcelain cabinet. There is nothing about Lady Louisa that challenges Ashmore. You, however—you'd do so nicely."

"No. You are mistaken! We don't get along at all. We fight the entire time. He disapproves of me! There is just something about his haughtiness that infuriates me. He'd be better off with Lady Louisa. They will never fight and live happily ever after with ten children."

"Fiddlesticks. Henry never used to be like that. David and Henry, they were two little hell boys when they grew up. Forevermore getting into trouble. When David died, he fell off that self-same roof that you so rashly attempted to climb yourself—something in Henry froze up. He retreated behind this shell of his. He drowns himself in work and duty. And he is overly protective of Arabella. He is stifling her. It isn't good for her. The best thing he did was send her to that school." The dowager sniffed. "It pains me to admit, but that place was good for her. Until you came along."

"See? I'm a disaster. Everyone is better off without me. Now, if you could help me convince the duke to write me a letter of recommendation, I will return to the Seminary and leave you all in peace and everyone will be happy again."

"Nonsense. Whatever on earth do you plan on doing at the Seminary? You don't intend to teach?" she cackled.

Lucy sat up straight. "Why, yes. That was the general idea."

"Nonsense. You'll be bored within a fortnight, after you have ruined the Seminary."

Lucy had the sinking feeling she wasn't entirely wrong.

"Last night was a tremendous mistake. It was a stupid thing to do. But I didn't know that his brother died like that. I would never have done it had I known. In any event, he doesn't really want to marry me." They were friends, maybe, and he had an obnoxious sense of duty that told her he needed to marry her. But there wasn't much more than that, was there? Then why did she feel so hopelessly confused?

"Be that as may. I've decided to keep you. You can either marry my grandson or you can become my companion. Make up your mind what it is to be."

"It is to be neither."

Lucy got up, curtsied stiffly and left the room, even though it was rude of her to leave before she was dismissed.

Lover's quarrel.

"Nonsense," she muttered to herself, but her heart leapt.

CHAPTER 18

*M*eg finished adjusting the hem of Lucy's ball gown. "How lovely you look, Miss."

It was Saturday, the day of the ball. She wore a white muslin gown with a low-cut bodice, embroidered at the hem with golden roses. Little curls framed Lucy's face and nervous excitement made her cheeks glow. It was her first real ball. The dancing evenings at the Seminary which Miss Hilversham had organised for practice didn't count. Would she remember the steps? She wished this evening were done and over with.

"If I may say so. Tonight, you will outshine even Lady Louisa." Meg pulled a crease out of the dress and looked satisfied.

"Fiddlesticks, Meg."

Meg grinned. "You sound like the Dowager Duchess."

"Alas." Lucy sighed. Meg was right. She'd turn into a crotchety old lady like the dowager if she didn't take care.

Lucy saw how Lord Blackmore raised his quizzing glass and watched her descend the stairs.

"Wouldn't call her a diamond of the first water, exactly, but otherwise she seems to be a decently fetching thing," she heard him say to Lord Rawleigh. "If one disregards her alarming tendency towards arithmetic."

"Eh." Rawleigh studied her from top to bottom. Lucy frowned as she dropped into a quick curtsy, then moved past them. "A bit too thin for my taste," he told Blackmore.

"I'll have to ask her to dance." Blackmore followed her into the ballroom.

Strains of music reached Lucy's ears. The musicians had started a quadrille, and the ballroom filled up quickly. Ashmore stood with his sister and the dowager by the ballroom entrance, greeting the guests. Arabella herself looked fetching in a cornflower blue gown that brought out the colour in her eyes. When acting in social functions, Arabella behaved with a natural, charming grace combined with a certain inborn pride that all Ashmores seemed to be born with.

But Ashmore! He took her breath away. He looked sinfully handsome. He was dressed smartly in a black tailcoat, knee breeches, white linen and an intricately tied neckcloth. He looked tall and proud, yet as he bent down to listen to Arabella tell him something, one of his rare smiles flitted over his stern features. Lucy's heart squeezed.

As if he'd read her thoughts, he looked up and their eyes met. The entire ballroom faded away and there was only him. Rooted at the spot, a sudden feverish flush spread through her. Her heart pounded, and her inside somersaulted. Lucy caught her breath and almost sat down on the bottom stair.

He nodded at her and she felt a happiness flush through her that left her confounded.

Then a vision in icy white approached him. Lady Louisa. He turned to her and held out his hand for the minuet.

She looked proud and triumphant. What a beautiful pair, Lucy thought.

"We're expecting an announcement tonight," Lucy heard the Duke of Tilbury, Louisa's father, mention to another guest.

Lucy exhaled shakily. She used all her willpower not to watch Ashmore and Lady Louisa.

"MAY I HAVE THIS DANCE?" MR GABRIEL STOOD IN FRONT OF her. She nodded and placed her hand in his. He was courteous and seemed to enjoy dancing with her. However, he didn't talk very much. Was he the man Arabella had lost her heart to? Arabella was always unusually animated in his company. She wondered why. Mr Gabriel seemed nice, but his character seemed somewhat mellow.

"Lady Arabella is very pretty tonight." She watched him closely.

"Indeed, she is." Mr Gabriel took her hand and led her around him in a circle. He'd not even looked at Arabella, who danced not too far away.

"I would say she is almost glowing with beauty."

"Very much so. I find all ladies here very beautiful."

Bah. She almost preferred Finbar's superficial flirtations over this.

"Yes, but Lady Arabella seems to exude something special tonight? I wonder what one could call it."

"It must be the light. This ballroom is fairly sparkling with all the candles that are lit."

Lucy gave up.

The dance ended, and Mr Gabriel bowed. Relieved, Lucy curtsied. She wanted to go to the refreshment room, but another gentleman stood in front of her for the next dance.

Lucy danced every single dance. Somehow, she never lacked a partner. Once, she saw Arabella dance with Mr Gabriel, and there were stars in her eyes and red spots on her cheeks. He looked at her with the polite interest that he gave all the other ladies.

Oh, no. Arabella was setting herself up for a heartache, Lucy thought.

Out of breath, Lucy curtsied to her partner, when Lord Blackmore asked her for the next dance. Lucy had never really liked him; he had a coarse sense of humour and his hands felt clammy and oily. She resisted the desire to let go of his hand and wipe it on her gown. Lord Blackmore gripped her hands too tightly and talked the entire time. Lucy had difficulty paying attention. Her mind was with Ashmore, who stood with Lady Louisa by the terrace doors. They looked so perfect together. A cold knot formed in her stomach. She knew Louisa expected a proposal tonight. She knew that Ashmore had intended to do precisely that. Until she came along.

She didn't know how she'd take it if Ashmore were to revert to his original plans and propose to Lady Louisa. The sharp jab twisting deeply into her heart implied that she probably wouldn't take it well at all.

"….five of them. She died with the sixth and alas, it didn't last beyond three days."

Goodness, what was that man talking about? She jerked her attention back to the present as she twirled about Blackmore's corpulent figure.

His wife. He'd been talking about his wife. And that she and the sixth child had died at birth. Poor thing.

"I'm terribly sorry." What an inane thing to say in the

146

middle of a dance. But she did feel sorry for him. He was a widower with five children. That can't be easy.

"Therefore, it seems expedient of me to remarry as soon as possible. A mother for the children, you see." The dance ended and Lucy sighed with relief. She wanted to curtsy and leave, but he kept holding on to her arm and propelled her towards the veranda. The doors were open and a fresh night breeze cooled Lucy's overheated cheeks. She hesitated, but a gulp of fresh air would be good for her. Ashmore was talking earnestly with Lady Louisa. What were they talking about? Lucy shifted uncomfortably.

".... don't you agree?"

Goodness, what had he said, again?

"Er, yes."

He beamed. "Excellent, excellent." They stood in front of the fountain. Lucy frowned. How had they ended up here? He must have manoeuvred her outside somehow. Blackmore advanced, and she retreated until she bumped against the stone façade of the fountain.

He emitted a slightly sickly sweet smell, mingled with sweat. Lucy backed sideways and rubbed her nose.

"Er, if you excuse me but, what did I just agree to? My mind has been wandering, you see."

"That is understandable. Nerves, yes?" He chuckled. "I have been saying that a young lady like you would be the perfect mother for my children. Robust enough to raise the bunch and young enough to bear some of her own."

Sweet heavens. Had he proposed marriage, and she'd missed it? She stared at him, speechless.

"Well, then?" He looked at her expectantly. "Can we announce our engagement?"

Lucy jumped. "Certainly not!"

"But Miss Bell. You as good as agreed to my proposal!"

"I did not!"

"Balderdash. Of course you did. Do I need to make myself clearer?" He grabbed her by the shoulders and smacked a kiss at the edge of her mouth. His breath smelled of cabbage.

A second later his head whipped back, he stumbled backwards over a root and crashed to the ground.

"The devil." Blackmore lay on the ground, stunned.

Lucy looked at the skinned knuckles of her fist. She unclenched her fist and rubbed her aching hand.

"That was a remarkably precise hit," said a voice with some hauteur. "I intended to come to the rescue, but I see that is unnecessary. You were not lying when you said you had a mean fist. Where did you learn how to hit like that?"

"At the Seminary, of course." She'd asked an errand boy to teach her.

"Of course. Why did I even ask?"

"Ashmore." Blackmore scrambled up. "I—she—we."

"There is no we. He tried to manhandle me, and I wouldn't let him." Lucy flexed her hand.

"Nonsense," Blackmore spluttered. "I merely tried to propose, and this is the answer I got."

"It is an unmistakably clear answer, Blackmore. Take it as a man."

"But Ashmore—"

"Are you hurt?"

"Yes," Blackmore replied. "My chin smarts."

"I wasn't asking you." Ashmore's voice could have frozen over the water in the fountain behind them.

Lucy shook her head. "I'm fine. I just didn't expect him to propose in this violent way. It was unexpected."

"Blackmore?" He whipped to attention. "Do you have anything to say to the lady?"

"What? Oh. Er. I wouldn't know what you mean."

"Think carefully, man, lest you find yourself with another planter, this time by me."

Blackmore goggled at the duke.

"But—But—"

Ashmore cracked his knuckles.

Blackmore paled.

"I beg your pardon, ma'am, for having offended you with my proposal and er— kiss."

"Keep a three-yard distance to her from now on. If I catch you encroaching on a space that is any less than that, you will answer to me personally."

Blackmore backed away. "I say. Ashmore."

"Is that clear?"

"Yes, sir. Three yards." He cleared his throat, straightened his coat and went back to the ballroom.

"In a way, I feel sorry for him." Lucy watched him retreat. "He seemed quite desperate to find a wife for his children."

"Yes. But not you." That came across as a command. Lucy's head whipped up. "You are too good for him."

"I am?" A wistful little smile flitted over her face. "If only that were so."

"Of course, you are. You have too low an opinion of yourself." He took her hand in his and inspected her knuckles. "This needs to be tended to."

"He has a head like granite," Lucy agreed.

He gently blew on her knuckles.

The little hairs on Lucy's neck stood on end. She held her breath.

The strings of the first waltz drifted out into the garden.

"Come dance with me," his voice was husky.

"I—am supposed to be dancing this waltz with Finbar," Lucy muttered, unable to tear her eyes from him.

"Hang Finbar." Ashmore drew her close, holding her right hand in his and placing his other hand on her shoulder.

He twirled her around under the cherry tree and Lucy felt she'd never experienced anything lovelier or more romantic.

He looked down on her, and there was something unreadable in his eyes.

For one moment she allowed herself to dream. What would it be like if she were his duchess? No Lady Louisa with land, no compromise, no honour-bound duty. What if he married her because he loved her? Maybe it could work. Maybe it wouldn't be so bad to be married to—Henry.

When the music ended, he still kept holding her in his arms.

Lucy lifted her face and she heard her voice say, huskily, dreamlike and disembodied: "I think I will kiss you."

She lifted herself up on her toes and pressed her lips against his. Warm, soft, spicy. It was perfect. Then she wanted to run, before her brain comprehended the full implications of what she'd just done. Again.

He drew her back to him. This time he took her face in his hands and lowered his lips to hers. It was not soft and gentle, but deep and urgent. His fingers caressed the silken skin of her nape.

Lucy trembled. She clung to him, kissing him back as if her life depended on it.

They were like two sides of the same coin, Henry and the duke. You couldn't love one without the other.

Then realisation hit her.

She'd been so busy hating him, that she hadn't realised she'd been yearning herself sick for this man with every fibre of her body.

Heaven help her, she was in love with Henry, the duke.

CHAPTER 19

*E*arly next morning, she sat up in bed as if hit by lightning.

Things were fairly simple when one wanted them to be. Why all this unnecessary resistance? Why continue to fight him? Whatever for? Engulfed in a fog of dreamy love and hope, she could hardly remember.

She'd marry Henry.

Because she loved him.

Whatever talk he'd spewed forth on honour because she'd been compromised—it was fustian. He just couldn't admit that maybe, deep down, he felt attracted to her as she did to him. Kisses didn't lie, did they?

She'd marry the duke, and it wouldn't be so bad to be a duchess, either, and she'd never have to worry about what to do with her life.

The dowager expected it. Arabella would be her sister. She'd have a proper family. A real home. Maybe children...

Lucy's world brightened. She scrambled up and grabbed the apple green muslin dress Meg had laid out for her.

She had to find Henry and tell him he should announce their engagement. Right now. Today.

She twirled. How wonderful life was!

Then Meg walked in.

"Oh, Miss Lucy, let me help you. Did you want to put this dress on?" She buttoned the little pearly buttons on the back. "That's a perfect dress for today, the weather's excellent for the village fair. You'll go, won't you, Miss?"

"There's a village fair?"

"Yes, Miss, it's been going on for days. I went there with my Pete on my day off. The plays are good."

"Oh? Who are the actors?"

"A funny name. Jolly something or other." Meg adjusted her dress. "You ought to have a look." She draped a green shawl over Lucy's shoulders.

Lucy didn't reply. She felt a chill sweep through her body.

"I say, Miss. You've gone awfully white. Maybe you should sit down?"

Lucy plopped down on a chair. "Jollyphus?"

"Yes, Miss." Meg poured a glass of water and handed it to her. "Something or other Jollyphus. It's a funny name. Jim and Jerry. Jem and Jelly."

"Joris and Jerry Jollyphus," Lucy whispered. She drank the glass of water in one gulp.

"Yes, that's it. Do you know them?"

"I've heard of them." Lucy set down the glass carefully. "A long time ago. When I was a child. You said they're performing at the village fair?"

Meg folded a dress and stored it in the chest. "Yes, Miss. There's something different every day. I might even go again and watch 'The Saucy Shepherdess' and 'Midsummer Night's Dream'. There's also a funny jester."

"Go with me."

"Miss?"

"Let's go together, Meg. I want to see them, too." Lucy got up, determined. "In fact, let's go right now."

"Where're you going?" Arabella suddenly stood in the room. Neither Lucy nor Meg had heard her come in. She looked at them curiously. "What are you cooking up now, Lucy? Can I join?"

"No! Under no circumstances."

"Miss. I'm expected to help Lady Louisa this morning." Meg pulled a face. "She's going through her entire wardrobe and needs my help."

"Whatever it is you're doing, I'm coming." There was a stubborn set around Arabella's mouth.

Lucy shook her head. "Ashmore won't like it."

"But, Lucy, Ash need not know. He's too busy with the guests here, and I'm bored. Grandmama is taking a nap, and Lady Louisa, as Meg says, is busy with her clothes. As are the rest of the ladies." Arabella looked at Lucy expectantly.

Lucy felt indecisive. Arabella probably wanted to make up after their fall-out. Lucy also felt guilty and owed her an explanation.

"Very well. But no one is to know."

"Where are we going?"

"To a fair."

"Splendid!" Arabella clapped her hands.

"A crowded, raucous village fair. There'll be pickpockets and all sorts of unsavoury people."

"Oh, I've never been to one! What a fantastic idea, Lucy. You always come up with the best ideas."

"If we go, we'll have to go in disguise. I don't want to be recognised as coming from Ashmore Hall. And let's not even think about what Ashmore will do when he discovers we've gone. You're supposed to be entertaining your guests, not sneaking off to the fair. It is very improper. Your brother will kill me if something happens to you."

"Forget about Ash. To the fair. In disguise. Meg, help me find some suitable dresses!"

The girls walked to the village across the field. The air was redolent of mutton pies, fricassee of chicken, custards, sweets and biscuits of all varieties. There were puppet shows, musicians, harlequins, and acrobats who juggled balls and spat fire.

Arabella was like a little child. She wanted to see and try everything and dragged Lucy by the arm from one booth to another. Arabella pulled Lucy to a sweets stand, where they bought two paper bags of sugared almonds.

Lucy didn't enjoy herself.

"I'm only interested in the theatricals. The travelling troupe of actors called Jollyphus," she explained as she bit into a rock-hard, sugar-coated almond.

"Oh look. Hot pie. Let's get some and then go into the mirror cabinet there."

Lucy sighed.

"I've never had such a good hot pie before," Arabella, who was used to caviar and truffle dinners, said with full mouth as she dragged Lucy to the mirror cabinet.

"There they are." Lucy almost gasped when she saw the worn down wagon with colourful drawings on the side. The faded, red letters *Jollyphus* were almost illegible. Above the name were drawings of two dwarves in harlequin costumes. Lucy pulled Arabella to the makeshift stage. The play was about to begin.

They watched the "Most Resplendid Drama of the Rise and Fall of the Queen of Atlantia," with a brief break, in which a jester entertained the group.

Afterwards, Lucy lingered as the crowd dispersed.

"Look, Lucy, there is a dancing bear over there." Arabella pulled at Lucy's arm.

"Go ahead, I'll wait for you right here. There's something I want to ask." Arabella was more than happy to wait as she watched the bear step on a tiny red ball without squashing it.

Lucy approached the pot-bellied man who seemed to be the head of the troupe.

"Excuse me, sir. I'd like to talk to the Misters Jollyphus, if you please."

He gave her a dismissive look. "Who's asking?"

Lucy hesitated. "A former friend."

He smacked his fat lips. "Not good enough." He turned and walked away.

"But sir—" Lucy started to go after him, when a voice stopped her.

"Lucibelle?"

She whirled. A lanky, red-haired man looked at her uncertainly.

Lucy stared.

"Phips?" she whispered.

"It really is you." A big grin spread over his face. "I'd recognise you anywhere, even though you're all grown up."

"So are you." The last time she'd seen Phips, he'd been a youth with pimples. "How are you?"

"Not too bad. Could be worse. Still travelling about. Still acting. Getting better. But look at you. All lady." He grinned.

Lucy teared up. "It's been so long."

Phips put his hands in his pocket. "Aye. Things've changed since you left."

Phips nodded at the pot-bellied man, who barked instructions at someone. "He ain't as good as Joris and Jerry, but he keeps the business running. There's no one left of the old troupe. Only me and Maia, and she quit the stage years ago. I still don't get to play Hamlet, but now and then they let me have the side roles."

"Joris and Jerry?" An icy hand squeezed her heart.

"Oh, no." He looked at the ground. "I thought you knew."

"Where are they?" She pulled him behind the wagon, out of the pot-bellied man's view. "What happened, Phips?"

"They—" He shook his head.

"Tell me. Where are they? They usually perform during the break, but I haven't seen them." Joris and Jerry had always been the real attraction.

"They're dead, Luce," Phips said gently.

"Dead." Lucy looked at him blankly.

"I'm so sorry. No one told you, then?"

She shook her head mechanically.

"There was a fire. At the inn where we stayed. We lost everything except for the wagon here. Joris and Jerry...they died in the fire. They were heroes. Rescued every single soul. When Joris didn't come out, Jerry went back in. Then neither came out again, and the entire structure collapsed. Right on top of them."

"When?" Tears glided down Lucy's cheeks.

"A while ago." Phips calculated. "Maybe five years."

"I didn't know. I didn't know." She grabbed his arm for support.

"No, you didn't. And how should you?"

"Where?"

"Up north. Near Inverness. They're buried there. The entire village came for their funeral."

Lucy cried into her hands. Phips gathered her in an awkward hug.

"Do they have a proper grave?" she asked after she cleaned her face with her sleeve.

"Aye, a nice, big one. Paid by the mayor himself."

"God knows when I'll get to visit it." Then she remembered Arabella. "I ought to go. I'm not alone."

"Before you leave, I've got something for you. From them. I kept it safe. Had it hidden under a board in the wagon so it didn't get lost. Wait here." He went to the wagon, rummaged underneath and pulled out a squashed, oblong tin box.

"It's for you, Lucibelle." He handed it to her. "Joris told me to keep it safe. For you. I think he knew he'd not see you again. He always knew these things, didn't he?"

Lucy took the box. "I had a feeling something must've happened. They used to write once in a while. Then they stopped. I could never write back because they were always on the move." She smiled bleakly at the memory.

"No, you were too busy in that school. They turned you into a lady, didn't they? But we always knew you were a princess. Joris and Jerry did the right thing by sending you there."

Lucy gave him a watery smile. "I loved them, but I also loved being at the Seminary. You know how I hated travelling around."

"And now? You still there?"

Lucy shook her head. "I'm staying at Ashmore Hall with my friend, Lady Arabella."

Phips whistled. "The duke's sister! You don't say. You've climbed into very elevated company, Lucibelle. And the duke, he's a high stickler if there ever was one. That steward of his called us gypsies and threw us off the land. We only camped on his meadow for a night."

Lucy sighed. "The duke can be—difficult. But he's not too bad. If you want, I can put in a word for you."

"Don't trouble yourself. We're staying at the inn. The innkeeper doesn't mind. Especially when things get merry in the evenings. On the duke's grounds, one has to behave all the time." He grinned again. "I'm thinking about settling down."

"What do you intend to do?"

Phips blushed furiously. "The inn I mentioned? There's a girl there. She said they need help."

"I'm happy for you, Phips. I hope it'll work out for you."

"Thank you." Then he looked serious. "Just one more thing. When you return to the 'nobs. Don't forget us, will you? Joris and Jerry. They were heroes. They deserve to be remembered. Never forget where you came from."

"I won't," Lucy choked. "I promise."

"Phips! Where's that boy when you need him?"

Phips looked over his back. "Prendergast. Joris and Jerry were worth ten times the likes of him. He's been in a foul mood the entire day."

Lucy wiped her nose and eyes and pulled herself together. "You'd better go. I don't want him biting your head off on my account."

"Blimey. It's time for me to leave this life, too."

"It's good talking to you again." Lucy remembered the gangly, tongue-tied boy that he used to be.

"Aye, it is."

She clasped her tin box. "I have to go, they'll miss me."

"Goodbye, Lucibelle. Godspeed."

"Goodbye, Phips." Lucy looked wistful as his red head disappeared between the wagons. He was the last link to a childhood she'd thought she'd all but forgotten.

CHAPTER 20

*A*rabella chattered about the afternoon's events the entire way back to the hall.

"I liked the bear most. Though the actors weren't bad, either. I think I'll ask Mrs Bates to serve us hot pasties for tea tomorrow."

"Why don't you go on ahead, Arabella? I'll join you shortly."

Arabella scrutinised Lucy's face. "Are you feeling quite well, Lucy? You've been unusually quiet."

"I'm not ready to face the company. I want to take a brief walk in the rose garden and think a bit."

"Very well." Arabella took a few steps, then stopped and turned. "You know, you could trust me with whatever is on your mind."

"Sometimes things are not so easy, Arabella."

"What's going on between you and Ash?"

Lucy swallowed and looked away. "With the episode on the roof, I've only proven his point that I'm irresponsible and up to no good. We argued. I apologised. That's all." She would not tell her about the kiss at the ball.

A look of guilt crossed Arabella's face. "It's also my fault. I could have told you about David. I didn't think."

"Yes. But that doesn't change the fact that he won't write me the letter for the Seminary."

"That is bull-headed of him. But there is more?"

Lucy shrugged. "Ultimately, it comes down to the fact that we just can't overcome our differences." That was an understatement, but the truth.

Arabella regarded her with a frown. "What about the man at the fair? Who gave you the box? I saw you talking to him. Was he the reason you wanted to go to the fair? I was hoping you'd tell me why."

"He's an old friend. That's all."

"I'm certain there's more to the story."

Lucy stared at the box in her hands. She wasn't ready to tell Arabella yet. Not when her mind was a whirl of sadness and confusion.

"Very well. I'll not push myself on you—or anyone, for the matter." Arabella set her jaw firmly. "Not anymore. I'm done with pursuing people for their friendship and affection. People who flatter me, flirt with me, are friendly and nice, but who will only ever see the duke's sister and not give a tuppence for who I really am."

Lucy smacked her head. "I'm such an idiot. Can you forgive me? Something has happened. Finbar? Gabriel? I will slaughter both of them with my bare hands."

"You always fight my battles, Lucy." Arabella shook her head so that her blonde locks flew. "I know you talked to Ash. He said he'll not pressure me into marriage with Finbar. It's to be my decision alone. I'm grateful for your intervention, but I don't want you fighting for me any more. I can stand up for myself. You're like Ash. Always protecting me. But neither of you really know what I want."

Lucy's eyes widened. "But Arabella. You always said you wanted to marry for love. That's what you wanted for all of us. And, that they are dukes." Lucy grimaced. "Wasn't that what the whole wishing well fiasco was about?"

Arabella smiled bleakly.

"Won't you tell me what's the matter?" Now it was Lucy prodding for more information.

"When you are ready to honestly talk about what's in your heart, then so am I." Arabella marched ahead.

Lucy quenched the urge to go after her. With a sigh, she watched her run down the hill towards the hall.

ASHMORE HALL BASKED IN THE GOLDEN GLOW OF THE SETTING sun. Lucy felt the familiar feeling of intimidation crawl over her. What had she been thinking? Marrying the Duke of Ashmore. Generations of Ashmores must turn in their graves at the very thought.

She sat down on the meadow and pried opened the lid of the tin box.

Inside was a frayed handkerchief, a few stones she'd liked to play with as a child, and a red button. She stirred in the contents with one finger. She barely remembered playing with those stones. They were unusually coloured river stones that must've delighted her as a child. The button she didn't remember. Had it been of her coat? And the handkerchief… it had a monogram on it, the initial S, which Joris and Jerry had firmly believed to be from her parents.

Her heart cramped up. So many hopes and dreams—for naught.

"It's a royal insignia. See?"

"One day your parents will find you. Then you'll live with them in your very own castle."

She'd believed them.

She'd believed them when they dropped her off at Miss Hilversham's, with a letter in her hand, signed by a non-existing Aunt Jemima. *"Because you need to get the education of a lady. You're a lady, a princess, you know."*

She'd believed every word. One day her parents would come and find her, and she'd live happily ever after with them. In her very own castle.

"You're meant for something better," Joris had told her.

Lucy dashed the tears away angrily with the back of her hand.

It was time to let go of those dreams.

Phips had been so right. She'd forgotten where she came from. Forgotten who she was. For she was not only an orphan, but a foundling with unknown roots, likely illegitimate, of working-class origins, raised on the dusty roads by a pair of travelling clowns.

Cruel voices had called them "dwarves".

"But that's nonsense, Lucibelle. We're just people of short stature," Joris used to say. "Always take pride in who you are."

Would Henry have accepted them? Or would his tolerance have reached his limit, here? Could he be that tolerant? He's a duke. A straight-laced high-stickler. He had a tremendous responsibility, a heritage to maintain. He liked to break out of his role, now and then, but he'd never subvert societal roles entirely by marrying so flagrantly beneath his station. Rash, irresponsible behaviour can lead to death. He disapproved of actresses, because one nearly ruined his father. He wasn't tolerant at all. Not when it came to actresses.

Lucy shivered.

Reality was, he had no idea how disreputable she was. She was a disastrous match for the duke. An alliance with her would, in all likeliness, ruin even him. She couldn't keep on deceiving him so grossly.

And Arabella? A deep sadness swept through Lucy. Arabella had always assumed Lucy was standing up for the lower classes out of the goodness of her heart. The reality was that Lucy was one of them. She'd ruin Arabella, too, if she married Ashmore.

CHAPTER 21

*A*shmore had ordered a picnic in the park the next day, because the weather was agreeable, to round off the week's events.

Dining alfresco was all the vogue, especially with silver platters, crystal chalices, silken napkins and Turkish carpets rolled out on the meadow. After having played lawn bowling, the game of graces, and shuttlecock, the ladies reclined on pillows under the cool shadows of the trees. The footmen, sweating under their wigs, carried heavy baskets stuffed with food. They served champagne in crystal glasses, dainty caviar canapes, eclairs, macaroons and dollops of syllabub in silver goblets.

What was missing, however, were the strawberries.

"A picnic without strawberries," complained Lady Bleckingham, as she fanned herself, for she was sweating profusely, "is like tea without milk."

"Or hunting without the deer." Lord Blackmore had recovered from the debacle at the ball and dug enthusiastically into the syllabub. He glanced at the older Stilton girl, who flushed scarlet. Lady Rawleigh had a smug face as she looked favourably on the pair. There would be a wedding soon.

"Or punch without the rum," Finbar hovered over Lady Louisa, who pretended to ignore him. Come and think of it, he was hovering quite a lot over Lady Louisa. Lucy observed them with interest.

And Mr Gabriel? He was oblivious to Arabella's yearning looks and conversed with Mr Fridolin about music.

Ashmore snapped his fingers, and three footmen jumped to attention. "Procure strawberries."

One of them—Felix—ran across the lawn.

Lucy shook her head in amazement. She sat on a carpet away from the group and had no appetite at all for any of the food.

"What is the matter, Miss Bell?" The duke sat next to her; one long leg stretched out. "I couldn't help but notice that underneath all your cheerfulness is a sense of melancholy." He looked at her searchingly.

It took Lucy a moment to recover from her surprise. Of all the people, it was the duke who'd seen behind her mask of happiness.

She swallowed the tears that threatened to well up and smiled. "I'm fine. Thank you for asking."

"Indeed?"

"Oh, yes. I was sad at some news that I received."

"Would you care to share it with me?"

"Well. I learned that some of my very dearest friends passed away." Blast those tears that threatened to spill out of her eyes. She wiped the corner of her left eye.

"My condolences. I'm so very sorry." He handed her his handkerchief.

She blew her nose, looked at the soiled handkerchief and laughed with a wobble, as she remembered the incident in the library. She kept the handkerchief. "It is more that this is so unexpected. A part of my childhood, of home, disappearing forever." She hadn't meant to say that, but there it was.

"They were childhood friends?"

Lucy hesitated. "Yes."

"It must be difficult to maintain a façade of jolliness when one is mourning."

Lucy jumped at the word "jolly." "Y–yes."

Part of her wanted to tell him about Joris and Jerry. How they'd raised her and how they'd done so gently and firmly, making sure, as she grew up, to receive the best education there was.

She didn't want to keep this a secret. She wanted him to know. She opened her mouth to tell him.

"There you are, Your Grace, I've been looking for you." Lady Louisa clamped her hand possessively around his arm. "We're rehearsing a play for tonight, and we need a fair judge." She pulled him away.

For once, Lucy was glad Louisa had interrupted.

It was best this way.

"Methinks the strawberries are approaching." Lord Conway shielded his eyes against the sun.

Felix the footman returned with a woman who scrambled after him. They each carried two baskets filled to the brim with strawberries.

"Your Graces, ladies and gentlemen, behold, the strawberries." To Ashmore in sotto voce, Felix said, "She insisted on delivering them herself, Your Grace."

The woman huffed and puffed in her excitement of finding herself in such elevated company. "From my very own garden. It is such an honour. You will see they are the sweetest, most delicious—oh!" The woman dropped the baskets and clapped her hands together. A look of ecstasy lit up her face. "Oh! It is you! Your Grace! Had I but known!"

The duke squirmed.

Lucy edged away and grabbed an empty basket to pull over her head. But it was too late. The woman had already seen her.

"And here is your lovely wife!" She could not have beamed more with delight. "So charming! Had I but known that it was you, the other day, and your wife—in my very own shed! What a tremendous honour! I shall tell my grandchildren about this. My great-grandchildren!"

Dead silence fell over the group.

"The devil. Ashmore? Tell us the woman is talking fustian." Tilbury, Lady Louisa's father, glowered at him.

"Wife?" Louisa squeaked as she pointed at Lucy. "She—is your wife?"

The duke closed his eyes. "I see an explanation is in order."

"By Jove's beard, Ashmore. That's the understatement of the century." A vein twitched in Tilbury's temple.

"Did she say shed?" Blackmore nearly burst with glee.

"If you will allow." Ashmore bit out. He pulled the struggling Lucy up beside him. "The woman is correct that Miss Lucy Bell is to be my wife. We have been, ah, secretly engaged to be married this past week. It is, er, a love match."

The scandalised silence stretched into infinity.

"Well. Bravo." The dowager finally said. "Felicitations are in order. Now that this is established, can we proceed to eating the strawberries?"

CHAPTER 22

*I*t was a nightmare.

Following the duke's announcement, chaos broke out. Tilbury exploded, Louisa fainted, Blackmore broke into raucous laughter, the ladies started talking all at once, Arabella jumped up and down, squealing, and Lucy— Lucy picked up her skirts and ran.

She flew past the gaping footmen, up the stairs to her room and locked herself inside, jumped into her bed and pulled the blanket over her head.

"Lucy. We have to talk." Ashmore rapped on the door.

"Leave me alone."

"I told you from the beginning that something like this would happen." He rapped again. "Blast it all, I wish it hadn't happened in this public and dramatic way, but it happened. There is nothing to be done about it. We have to go through it. Open the door." He sounded grimly determined.

"Please, please, please go away." Lucy pulled the pillow over her face.

There was a muffled curse, then footsteps.

Another knock, this time more timid.

"Lucy. It's me." Arabella. "I just wanted you to know—it's really fantastic! You and Ash! It's the most wonderful thing! I understand now why you felt you had to keep it a secret. How I'd love having you as a sister, an actual sister! I'm so happy! But do open the door and talk to Ash? And look, little Bart is here, too."

Lucy heard the little dog yipping and scratching at the door.

"She misses you, poor thing."

Lucy could resist Ashmore and Arabella, but she couldn't resist Bart. She opened the door a gap for the puppy, when a boot wedged itself in and Ashmore pushed the door open.

He picked up the puppy, pressed it into Arabella's hands, then shut the door behind him and leaned against it with crossed arms. "Time to talk."

Lucy backed up until her legs hit the box in front of the bed. "Listen, I've thought about it. The best thing is for me to disappear and you tell them you changed your mind and it was all a colossal mistake. Yes, there will be a scandal for a while—very well—so there will be a rather enormous scandal—but it's nothing you won't survive. In a year it'll be old news. You're big and important enough, and the Ashmore name is untouchable. Your word is law, and if you insist it was all a misunderstanding and that nothing scandalous ever happened, everyone will just forget about it in a jiffy. I'll just disappear, and they'll forget about me. I promise."

"Is the thought of being married to me so repugnant to you?" His smile was bleak.

Lucy shook her head. "You don't understand."

He threw up his hands. "You're right. For the life of me, I don't understand. I certainly don't understand why you'd throw yourself at a gardener but refuse the proposal of a duke. Do you care to explain?"

"Look. Look who I am." Lucy picked up the small box, opened the lid and showed him the scrubby contents.

Henry took the box. "A few stones, a button, a theatre programme of a travelling troupe and a handkerchief." He fingered the handkerchief and frowned. "How is this relevant to the topic at hand?"

"This is evidence of my background. The only evidence of my birth. I'm a foundling. They found me in an open grave when I was two. No one knows how I got to be there, or who my parents were. I'm probably illegitimate. I'll never know. They raised me in a travelling troupe. On the streets. I spent my entire childhood travelling. Acting. Singing. My fathers wanted more for me and sent me to Miss Hilversham's Seminary to receive a proper education."

"Fathers?" He narrowed his eyes.

"Joris and Jerry Jollyphus. You may have heard of them. They were—we were—a very popular travelling troupe. They died in a fire," Lucy choked. "I only learned of that yesterday. After the incident with the wishing well—you were so furious about it, remember? Miss Hilversham sent me away, to a position as a governess. After two years I left because the son of the house assaulted me."

"By God. Did he hurt you?" He set his jaw.

"No. I hurt him." She showed him her fist. "Afterwards, I ran away to London. To a world I'm familiar with. Drury Lane. I sold oranges and flowers there. One day, they needed someone to jump in for a minor side role. They took me. I've been acting ever since."

He shook his head as if not comprehending.

"I've been on a public stage with Harriet Westington, Henry. *The* Harriet Westington. Not only am I base-born, growing up on the streets of England, I'm a second-rate actress." Her voice thickened. "I'm everything you ought not to be marrying."

"Why the blazes didn't you tell me before? Why all the lying?"

"Why didn't you tell me who you were when we first met? Why the secrecy?" she shot back.

He raked his hand through his hair. "This is an entirely different matter."

"No, it isn't. It's exactly the same. Tell me, Your Grace. Why you didn't reveal the secret of who you were when we first met." How long ago that seemed.

He closed his eyes. "I enjoyed the freedom of being gardener Henry."

"Exactly. I enjoyed the freedom of just being Lucy. Arabella's friend. Not Lucibelle Bellini of the disreputable world of acting."

"Lucibelle Bellini. Good God."

"My stage name."

He shook his head in disbelief.

"This here," she pointed at the box, "summarises what I am. The stones—the toys of my childhood. The theatre programme—how I was raised. The handkerchief—probably stolen from someone—sometimes they steal from the audience—to comfort a crying girl, to tell her it's proof that her origins are genteel. It's a lie I've believed my entire life, but no more. The fact is this: you can't marry me. I'm an actress. You hate actresses."

He didn't reply.

Lucy's heart ached. She wanted to memorise his face. That stern jut of his chin. His proud mouth and aquiline nose. She wished she could throw herself at him. Hold him. Feel the constant beat of his heart. Forever. She clung to the edge of the furniture to prevent herself from doing precisely that.

He rubbed his hand over his face. "What an unutterable mess this is."

"By now you should know that I have a talent for making messes."

There were worlds between them. A yawning chasm that could never be bridged. The duke, on the top of the aristocratic ladder, and she, on the very bottom, lumped together with other Drury Lane doxies. It was impossible. It was a fact of life, yet it hurt.

He paced. He stopped, raked his hand through his hair, and glowered at her. "You made a world-class fool of me."

"Yes," Lucy whispered.

He resumed pacing. "But what is the alternative?" he muttered to himself.

Lucy's heart wept. "There is no alternative. It's like I said. The best move is that I disappear." She went to the wardrobe and took out her carpetbag.

He watched intently.

"Hang it all. It's no use."

Lucy's head snapped up.

He stood in the middle of the room, his hands against his hips, looking at the ceiling, an odd smile playing about his lips. "I've been an ass. They can all go to blazes. It doesn't matter what they say. None of it matters."

Lucy wondered if he had lost his mind.

He stepped forward and took her ice-cold hands between his warm ones. "Lucy." She saw the heart-rending tenderness of his gaze. Her pulse skittered alarmingly.

"It matters. It matters very much. Otherwise you are repeating the same mistake as your father," she babbled and backed away.

"I'm not my father," he growled as he followed.

"You are about to make the same mistake."

"My father had no inkling what love really meant."

Lucy gasped as the full implication of his words hit her.

173

"Lucy—" He moved to pull her to him, but she wound herself away and fled behind a chair.

"Please don't say it." She put both hands over her ears.

He kicked the chair away and drew her up against him. Her heart thundered.

"I will say it. And you will listen. You know I've loved you since you first climbed on that blasted cart."

"No, no." She shook her head. Tears welled up in her eyes. "You don't know what you are saying."

"Of course I know." His eyes lit up with an inner blaze. "I know that only love matters and to hell with the rest."

"You can't do this. You have responsibilities. Duties."

"They can go hang for all I care."

"This is not the Ashmore I know."

"Ashmore is a fake. He doesn't really exist and you, my beautiful, wild, wonderful Lucy, were the first and only person to realise that." He laughed, as if freed from invisible iron shackles. "You have helped me see the truth of who I really am."

"No. Please. I beg of you, let it be."

He dropped his hands. "I'm too old for you. You should have a season. Is that what you want? I would wait for you, if you wanted that."

She shook her head and said thickly, "I don't want a season and you are not too old."

"I've never been in love before, Lucy. Not like this. And I know, despite your resistance, that you are not indifferent to me." His voice was hoarse.

She choked up. "I'm not even fit to be a gardener's wife, and you know it." Why wouldn't he see reason?

"Quit putting yourself down."

She forced herself to harden up, retreat deep inside herself behind a shell. "It is true. Do you know how many disreputable proposals I receive in London, after I have been on stage? Almost daily. They were outbidding each other." Her voice turned hard. "Now, if you were to join the ranks of the bidders, I might consider it." She felt her lips twist into a cold smile.

Henry recoiled. "You misunderstand. I am not offering for you to be my mistress, but my wife."

A stony mask slid over her face. "I would be better off as your mistress. If you can outbid the Duke of Malwich, who offered quite a considerable sum, jewellery and a house in the bargain."

His cheeks flushed. "Stop talking like that, it doesn't become you."

"You'd better get used to it because that is how we talk, we actresses. Your father would have been familiar with that kind of talk."

"Why are you like this, Lucy? I offer you my heart and marriage, and you throw it back in my face?"

The look of pain in his eyes nearly broke her, but she held on to the last remnants of her strength. "Because, maybe, I don't want marriage but freedom. Freedom of the stage, with all its glitter, glory, fame, and money. It's amusing to have the powerful dukes of the realm bid over my favours. Why tie myself down to only one? You think you know me. But you don't. And lastly, you've forgotten one thing." She drew a shaky breath before delivering the killing thrust. "I don't love you. Sure, I was fond of Henry the gardener. But the duke? Not nearly enough to fetter myself to a lifetime of boredom and duty."

Henry's face went stark white. "I see," he said after a long and heavy pause. He nodded once, as if he ought not to be surprised at this revelation. "Then there is nothing left to be said." For a flicker of a second, Lucy saw bleak anguish in his eyes. Then his gaze shuttered, and he instantly transformed back into the marbled ice duke. "Forgive my imposition on your time. Your servant, ma'am." He bowed stiffly.

Lucy closed her eyes to shut out that vision. "I apologise for everything, Your Grace. Please believe me, none of this was my intent. The scandal will blow over eventually. I never intended to hurt or harm anyone." She suppressed a sob. "Least of all you."

But he'd already left the room.

CHAPTER 23

SEVERAL MONTHS LATER. MISS HILVERSHAM'S SEMINARY, BATH.

*L*ucy saw the engagement announcement in *The Times.*

She shouldn't have been so surprised. After all, it was to be expected.

She stared blindly at the striped wallpaper until the maid asked her, timidly, whether she should take the tea service away since her tea had gone all cold.

"Yes please, Martha." Lucy took a shaky breath and folded the newspaper into smaller and smaller squares.

The Duke of Ashmore and Lady Louisa Whitehall would live happily ever after. It was best like that. Really. For everyone involved.

She swallowed and swallowed, but hot tears spilled onto her cheeks.

Blast and drat.

There was a quick knock on the door, and Pen stuck in her head. "They're waiting for you in the classroom."

"I'll be along in a minute." Lucy scrubbed the tears away with her hand. Pen hesitated, then went over to her. Wordlessly, she knelt down next to Lucy's chair and laid her head on her lap. Lucy choked. She put her hand on Pen's black hair. She understood it was Pen's way of comforting her.

"I've a class to teach," she said after a while.

Pen nodded and got up. At the door, she startled Lucy when she said, fiercely, "I would just go to him."

"But he's to be married."

Pen shrugged. "Only love matters."

She left, leaving Lucy wondering what exactly Pen knew about love. She was the youngest in their group, but sometimes, she seemed wise beyond her years.

MISS HILVERSHAM HAD BEEN RELIEVED WHEN LUCY SHOWED up on her doorstep. She'd taken the girl into her arms and held her tightly. Her eyes brimmed with tears, but maybe it was just the spectacles glinting in the sun.

"I've been reproaching myself every day this last year, Lucy," Miss Hilversham held onto Lucy's hands as if afraid she'd lose her again. "I was so worried when I learned that you ran away from your position. I knew something must've happened. For a while, I told myself that maybe you'd run to your aunt. But then, I suspected that your aunt didn't really exist. Why did you never tell me? All those years." She shook the girl by the shoulders. "You should have told me."

"I—I was afraid that you'd send me away. How did you discover that Aunt Jemima didn't really exist?"

Miss Hilversham sighed. "There were so many signs. She never wrote. She never visited. That alone should have been a red flag. Then, the payments stopped."

"But that means—that means—" She dropped her head in her hands. Her eyes widened as she understood. "All this time you didn't receive any payment, but you let me stay on."

Miss Hilversham had never revealed Lucy was a charity student.

She threw herself in Miss Hilversham's arms again and cried. After she finished, Miss Hilversham tucked the wet strains of her hair behind her ear. "And now, Lucy. Tell me exactly what happened. Tell me your story from beginning to the end."

Lucy wiped her nose. "The entire story?"

"The entire story." Miss Hilversham looked her usual severe self again.

"So, you are Lucibelle Bellini." Miss Hilversham shook her head in amazement. "You made it on the stage with Harriet Westington. Why didn't you stay there? You could have had a successful career as an actress?"

Lucy, who was sitting on a footstool next to Miss Hilversham's chair, leaned her head against her armrest. "Because I hated every minute of it," she whispered. "Because fame really means nothing. I wasn't meant to be for the stage. Joris and Jerry realised that. That is why they sent me here. Oh, Miss Hilversham, I was so homesick. All I wanted was to come back and—just be here. But I thought I needed the duke to write a letter so you'd take me back."

"You silly child. I never needed any letter to convince me to take you on as a teacher. You can stay here for as long as you want, Lucy."

"Thank you." Lucy got up.

Lucy had achieved what she wanted. She was back at the Seminary. Yet things were not as they used to be. So much at the Seminary had changed. Arabella was in Ashmore Hall and wrote weekly letters, at first eagerly, then when Lucy didn't reply, she gradually stopped. Birdie had moved on to a position as a governess. Pen was still here, watching Lucy with her troubled eyes, not speaking much.

It was good to be home, Lucy told herself.

"MISS BELL, MISS HILVERSHAM IS EXPECTING YOU IN HER office." Martha, the maid, interrupted Lucy's reverie. She was supposed to be grading essays; however, she'd been staring a hole into the wall for the past half an hour.

"I'm not ready for visitors." She wore a wrinkled afternoon dress, had ink stains on her fingers and her hair was dishevelled. "Who is it?"

"I don't know, Miss. They said they'd wait if you were in class."

Lucy sighed. It was probably some students' parents. She'd had more than one meeting like that.

For one moment she allowed herself to daydream that it was Henry. Her heart pounded.

No. How could the mere thought of Henry put her in such physical agitation? It was time to forget him, once and for all.

She straightened her dress and tucked a loosened hair strand behind her ear. This was the best she could do for now.

MISS HILVERSHAM, PERCHED BEHIND HER DESK, LOOKED UP, bespectacled and proper. "Lucy, come in. There is someone here to see you. Lord and Lady Sullivan, this is Lucy Bell."

A lady, with a hat of white satin and ostrich feathers, sat in a chair by the window. A gentleman with iron grey hair stood next to her. Lucy didn't recognise them.

"Good afternoon."

The couple stared at Lucy as if she were one of Lord Elgin's marbles on the exhibit. She self-consciously smoothed down her crumpled dress and wished she'd changed into a fresh dress.

"Hector." The lady held out a gloved hand to the gentleman who took it. With the other, she covered her mouth.

The gentleman's eyes widened.

Lucy looked from one to another. An odd feeling took hold of her.

The lady got up and took Lucy's hand and pulled her to the window. "The spitting image," she said with wonder.

"Who are you?" Lucy's heard her own voice come from far away, like from a dream. An old childhood dream.

"Twenty-one years ago, on April 1st, we had a daughter, Hector and I. We christened her Catherine Elisabeth. She was a cheerful little baby with chubby cheeks. Little Cathy was always happy." Her voice had a hitch. "The nurse—a Mrs Susan Billings, was a reliable woman, or so we thought." The lady's face crumbled.

The gentleman stepped over to her. "We had no reason to doubt Mrs Billings, at first."

The lady pulled herself together. "She seemed to be a most excellent nurse. Little Cathy thrived." Her voice wobbled. "But we were mistaken. So mistaken! Mrs Billings, contrary to outward appearance, was an unstable, mentally sick woman. We don't understand what happened, but one day, when Cathy was two, she simply took her." Her mouth worked as if it was a chore to utter those words. "She took Cathy out of the nursery and left the house. She was seen walking with our daughter in her arms along the road to Hamborough village. We never saw either of them again."

The lady, in agitation, pulled out a handkerchief and dabbed the corner of her eyes.

"The handkerchief—" Lucy's eyes burned into it. It had the same monogram as hers. She'd lost it after her last encounter with Henry, so she could not produce it.

"In other words, your child was kidnapped by her nurse." Miss Hilversham tapped the tip of her quill on the table. "The question is: why?"

"We will never know the true reason, Miss Hilversham." The gentleman never took his eyes off Lucy. "The bow street runners found the woman at the London docks two years later, impoverished, drunk, and feeble of mind. When questioned, she admitted she had taken Cathy, but she swore on her life she was her child. Apparently, she'd lost her own child previously. It was impossible to get more out of her. Her mind was completely gone. She barely knew her own name. She couldn't say what happened to Cathy, though it seemed likely that she must have abandoned her somewhere." The man's voice filled with anguish. "We had the entire countryside searched up and down, no result. The woman was sent to gaol in Newgate, where she died a few days later. We continued searching, but to no avail. By Jove, how we searched. All those years. We didn't leave a corner of England unturned."

Lady Sullivan spoke directly to Lucy. "Until last week. We received an—anonymous communication that the person we're looking for might be here at this Seminary. We came, certain it was yet another dead end. Then you entered the room."

"An anonymous communication? Who could that be?" Miss Hilversham frowned.

"It matters not." Lord Sullivan brushed it aside. "What matters is that we may have our first real lead to a successful end of our search. We may have found our daughter."

"Why are you certain Lucy is your daughter?" pressed Miss Hilversham.

Lady Sullivan looked into Lucy's eyes. They were the same limpid grey as hers.

Lord Sullivan was visibly moved. "We have a portrait hanging in our drawing room. It is of my wife's mother when she was a young girl. It is as though you'd stepped out of it."

"You are the spitting image of my mother, child." Lady Sullivan asserted. "But tell me one thing. Cathy had a mole in the shape of a strawberry between her shoulder blades."

Miss Hilversham got up, stepped up to Lucy and pulled down the top edge of the dress. She showed it to the couple. The mole was there.

"It looks like your parents have found you, Lucy."

Lucy's world tilted. This was a dream, she told herself. Her childhood dream materialised. It wasn't real. It couldn't be. It was impossible.

She pinched herself.

The lady's grip was firm, as she led Lucy to a chair. "Tell me about yourself."

Lucy told them. The entire story of her childhood, how the Jollyphuses had found her in the graveyard, how she'd grown up with the travelling troupe, how she travelled up and down the country, performing with them.

Shattered, the man hid his face in his hands. "Good heavens. Little Cathy in an open grave. And a travelling troupe. That explains why you were so difficult to find. Always on the move."

"My child. What you must have suffered." The woman wept.

Lucy went up to her, not knowing whether to comfort her. "In truth, the Jollyphuses treated me well. They were like fathers to me, both of them. I loved them d-dearly. But Jerry always believed—he always told me that in reality I was—a princess. I used to believe him. He'd invented this story of me being the child of a royal couple, and that one day they would find me. It was my favourite story. And now, can it really be true?" She stared at them, Lord and Lady Sullivan. Strangers. Could they really be her parents?

The woman smiled at her tremulously; the man rubbed his neck.

All of them got up at the same time. Lucy took a step forward and somehow found herself surrounded by two pairs of warm arms.

"Daughter. We have found you."

CHAPTER 24

A YEAR LATER. SULLIVAN HALL, SUSSEX.

Sullivan Hall was lovely during the summer. Lucy walked through the rose garden, which was not as big as the one at Ashmore Hall. The roses reminded her of Henry.

A year had passed since she'd last seen him. He must be married by now. Maybe he even had a child.

Lucy plucked the dead petal off a rose and let it float to the ground.

She enjoyed living with her parents, Lord and Lady Sullivan, who spoiled her at every turn. It was a dream come true. She even had a brother, Charlie, three years younger than her, who liked to tease her playfully.

Sometimes, Lucy woke up in the night, thinking it was all a dream, that she was still lying in the wagon's corner as it rumbled along the dusty country roads. Or sometimes she awoke, full of panic that she was missing her performance on stage.

She didn't miss the theatre.

She didn't even miss the Seminary, even though she'd enjoyed her short teaching stint there. Sometimes she thought of continuing in that profession, even though it was no longer required of her, nor even proper of her, to work. She would never have to earn her livelihood again. Her parents wanted a season for her. She'd declined, and they understood. Even if she never married, she'd be well off.

She thought of travelling. Lucy plucked another leaf off the rose. She had loads of money, now. She could travel the world three times over, if she wanted. Yes. Maybe she should do that. Leave England. Go to India, Egypt, the West Indies. Anywhere but here.

Guilt rushed through her. Was she entirely maggot-headed? Her entire life she'd yearned for a family, for a home. Now she finally had it, and she wanted to leave? Someone needed to open her head and check what was wrong with her brains.

Though she suspected it was not her head, but her heart that ailed rather badly.

"Cathy, dear." Her mother joined her and drew her arm through hers. She called her Cathy and Lucy was fine with that. New life—new name. Let the old Lucy Bell die, just as Lucibelle Bellini had died. Now she was The Honourable Catherine Elizabeth Edgewood, daughter of Viscount and Viscountess Sullivan.

"Come, let's sit here." She pulled Lucy on the stone bench next to the yellow rosebush. "I know we agreed to postpone your season for a while, so I do not want to press you on this matter. We have, however, received an invitation that is not judicious to decline. One does not rebuff invitations from certain people."

"Did the king send you a personal invitation?" Lucy's lips formed the ghost of a smile.

"No. But the Duke of Ashmore did. For his annual house party."

"No." Lucy's lips lost all colour. She stood up. "If you don't mind, Mother, I'd rather not go there." Over her dead body. Even her corpse would resist if it ever came to that.

"I know, child, last summer you spent some time there, and you didn't part well with his sister." That was the story she'd told them. They didn't know half of it. "However, we cannot turn down an invitation from one of the most powerful men in the country. Your father has some political issues to discuss with him. This would be an excellent occasion for him to do so. And for you, it would be an opportunity to make up with your friend." She searched Lucy's face, which had shut down completely. "You and Lady Arabella were rather close once, Miss Hilversham told us."

"Please believe me, the rift is entirely insurmountable." Lucy clutched at the side of her skirt. Her mother didn't know the entire story. She couldn't tell her, either. She felt a deep pain in her heart every time she thought of her time at Ashmore Hall.

Lucy could be obnoxiously hard-headed, but she'd inherited that from her mother, who was even more hard-headed than Lucy.

Lady Sullivan set her lips firmly. "It would please us both, myself and your father, not to mention your brother, Charlie, to accept the invitation and go to Ashmore Hall. We won't leave you behind. I'm afraid you really have no choice and you will have to, no matter how difficult, overcome your reluctance and join us with as much goodwill as you can muster. Come, child," she softened, "you'll see, it won't be so bad."

Lucy looked at the stubborn set of her mother's chin and realised she'd finally found her match. Her stomach dropped all the way to the gravelled path.

She would see Henry again.

In married bliss to his wife Louisa. With maybe a child or two.

She'd rather be dead.

LUCY FELT INCREASINGLY QUEASY THE CLOSER THEY approached Ashmore Hall. A minute ago, they'd passed the little brook where she'd fished out Bartimaeus. At least the puppy was something to look forward to.

None of them knew about Lucy's new identity. What would they think? She'd left in disgrace as Lucibelle Bellini. She'd lied to them. Deceived them. Left a massive scandal in her wake. Now she was returning as The Honourable Catherine Edgewood. She expected the entire assembly from last year to be there. Lord and Lady Rawleigh, Lord Blackmore, the Stiltons. Lucy groaned. They would snub her and frown at her, and her entire family would be in disgrace.

The carriage turned into the magnificent alley that led straight up to the proud house. The path was lit with torches and all the windows seemed to be ablaze with light. Lucy wiped her cold and clammy hands on her pink carriage dress, wrinkling it. She felt nauseous with nervousness.

The carriage drove up to the house and stopped. Footmen rushed forward, opened the doors, pulled out the stairs. Her parents and brother descended first, then Lucy tripped down the steps.

Heaven help her. All the Ashmores were standing in front of the house. Lucy wanted to pick up her skirts and run all the way back to Sullivan Hall.

The dowager braved the night air and stood leaning on her cane; a thick shawl draped around her shoulder. Arabella, as beautiful as always, bobbed up and down in excitement.

And him.

Her heart stopped.

He stood tall and immobile; his hands clasped behind his back.

Stiff, buttoned-up, proud and haughty.

Forevermore the Duke of Ashmore.

Their eyes met.

Lucy wished for nothing more in the world than a hole to open up in the ground so she could sink into it and never emerge.

Her father was talking, her mother was talking, Arabella was talking and laughing and clasping her into her arms. "Lucy, finally! How pretty you look. How dare you not reply to all my letters, you terrible girl?"

Lucy was in a daze. What, none of them were surprised to see her? They all accepted without question that she stepped out of this carriage in a tremendously expensive dress, calling herself The Honourable Catherine Edgewood? Almost as if they'd expected it?

"Well. It's about time." The dowager patted her arm, which confused her even more.

Her gaze fluttered from person to person and arrested when it reached him.

He bowed to her in that abrupt manner of his. "Miss Edgewood."

That was all.

She bobbed a quick curtsy. Lucy could not, for the life of her, find even a single word to say.

They were all ushered into the drawing room.

"Where is everyone else?" Lucy asked Arabella.

"Who do you mean?"

"All the other guests?"

A look of understanding dawned in Arabella's eyes. Her lips formed a round O. "You thought this would be a big house party? But no. It is just you, your brother and your parents. Isn't this grand? I'm so excited. I can't wait for you to tell me the complete story. It's better than a fairy tale."

"But where is Her Grace?"

Arabella looked at her uncomprehendingly. "Grandmama is over there."

"I mean—Louisa."

"Louisa? She's in London. I wrote in one of my letters that she got engaged to Lord Finbar. Didn't you get my letters? They're to have a grand wedding at the end of summer. London is talking of nothing else."

Lucy sat down heavily on the blue settee. "I thought—I thought…" She shook her head as if to clear it from fog. "Never mind."

Henry hadn't married Lady Louisa Whitehall.

That was the only thing that was going around in her mind right now.

She looked at him, standing by the fireside, conversing easily with her father.

Arabella kept talking, her cheeks flushed, her face animated. It occurred to her she didn't look heartbroken at all that Finbar married Louisa.

"And you? How do you feel?" Lucy interrupted her stream. "About Finbar and Louisa, I mean."

Arabella shrugged. "She can have him with my blessing."

Lucy bent towards her. "And Mr Gabriel?"

"He married the older Stilton sister, Emma, at the end of the summer." Arabella looked away.

"Oh, Arabella. I'm so sorry." Lucy took both her hands in hers. "I've been a terrible friend."

Arabella looked at her seriously. "You could have trusted me."

"I know." Lucy whispered. "I feel I don't deserve your friendship. All the lies I told. I've been far too self-absorbed and never really noticed what you went through. Can you ever really forgive me?"

"Lucy. You are such a goose. I'd very much like to go and visit you at Sullivan Hall, but I daresay you have other plans now."

Lucy wanted to ask what she meant, when she was interrupted by a yipping black arrow shooting through the room straight towards her.

It was Bartimaeus.

"Bart, Bart!" Lucy picked up the licking, squiggling bundle. She was bursting with health. "How you have grown!"

"This pup gives us all sleepless nights." The dowager sniffed, but there was a fond undertone in her voice. "She insists on sleeping in all our rooms, preferably Ashmore's, and if she doesn't get her way, she yowls and wakes up the entire house. I daresay it is our own fault, and the servants' as well—particularly Meg's and Felix's—since we're to use names, aren't we—for having spoiled her rotten. There isn't a more spoiled dog in the entire kingdom, even though Henry attempts to train her. Without success, I may add."

Bart clawed her way onto Lucy's lap and licked her hands. Lucy kissed her nose, picked her up and went to the veranda.

"So, you have been misbehaving, Bart? How terrible of you. I'll take you outside so you can run around on the grass."

She walked down the stairs and set her on the grass, where Bart sniffed out the insects.

"Well, Lucy." Lucy jumped and whirled around to face Henry, who was watching her. "Or rather, Miss Edgewood. Catherine. I heard that is your new name now."

"My parents call me Cathy. But Lucy will do."

"Yes. To me, you will always be Lucy."

Feeling out of her depth, she didn't know what to say.

"Shall we take a walk? The rose garden is particularly lovely this season." He offered her his arm, and she took it. They were as formal as a pair of strangers.

The roses smelled fragrantly in the summer night.

"I shall have to plant new roses over here. Either the hybrid tea rose, or the floribunda rose. What do you think? It would form a nice nook. With a little bench in the middle."

He was talking of roses. Really?

"I heard you didn't marry Lady Louisa after all. I—I saw the engagement announcement."

"Hm. Yes." He bent to fiddle around with a rose stem. "After the fiasco last summer, and your sudden disappearance, her father was overly eager to seal the union, so he sent the announcement to the paper, thinking that would settle things. Alas, he hadn't counted on his daughter."

Lucy looked at him, confused. "Why?"

"She discovered something—shall we say—unsavoury about me."

"Unsavoury?" What on earth was he talking about?

"Well, yes. She discovered my secret vice. My penchant for dressing up in poor gardener's clothes and spending the greater part of my day mucking around in the dirt. I insisted on wearing my gardener's garb for an entire afternoon. She walked in on me here, in the rose garden. Smoking my pipe."

"Oh. She was probably shocked?"

"Excessively so. She considered me to be ungentlemanly and vulgar." He paused to consider. "She's right, of course. But I found I didn't care a tuppence about her opinion."

Lucy chuckled.

"Miss Edgewood." Their eyes met.

"It's incredible, I know," Lucy babbled on. "I was afraid that you'd accuse me of dissembling again. You know. My history of acting. But the truth is that my parents turned up at Miss Hilversham's one afternoon." Lucy shook her head. She still didn't grasp how things had turned out.

"And you never asked why?"

"They say an anonymous letter—I thought that maybe Phips from the Jollyphuses—" she looked at Henry, who smirked. Lucy gasped. "It was you! But how? But why?"

He pulled out a handkerchief from his pocket. "You kept so many of my handkerchiefs, I thought it was my turn to keep one of yours." He handed it to her.

"You have it! I thought I'd lost it! But when…" her voice trailed away as she remembered the painful last meeting they had, where she'd shown him the box—with the handkerchief. He'd taken it along.

"The monogram. Why didn't it occur to you to investigate it, silly girl? I gave it to Brown, and he discovered the family within two days. I daresay I knew you were Miss Catherine Edgewood long before you did."

She shook her head, dazed. "I was convinced Joris just happened to come by the handkerchief, that it had nothing to do with my identity. It would've been too disappointing otherwise, you see."

"I wrote the Sullivans a letter, telling them about you. Three days later, Lord Sullivan knocked on my door."

"It wasn't an anonymous letter, like my parents say?" Lucy said.

"Not at all. I blackmailed him rather badly, poor man."

"Blackmail?"

"Hm. Yes. I told him I'd tell him of his daughter's where-abouts only if he gave me his permission to marry her. It was a tough negotiation. He wanted three years alone with his daughter before he'd see her married. I bargained it down to a year. That year is up now."

He took a step closer. He was so close; she could smell his cologne. Lucy pricked herself on a rose. A drop of blood formed on her forefinger. She pulled her hand away, but Henry took it.

He wiped her finger with the handkerchief and kissed it. Then he kissed her palm.

Heat sparked from where his lips touched her skin, spreading throughout her body, consuming her.

"But—after all the terrible things I said to you?" Lucy had difficulty keeping her voice steady.

"After our argument, I went out gardening, to work off my frustration. It occurred to me, far too late, for you were long gone, that maybe you were trying to give me a disgust on purpose, to drive me away. And, fool that I was, I'd believed it. I realised that that'd be something so like my Lucy to do. Stubborn, big-hearted, generous to a fault, my Lucy sacrificing her own happiness because she felt she wasn't good enough to deserve it. To put herself down for those she loves most. Am I right? Tell me I am right?"

His eyes burned into hers. Hopeful and fearful at the same time.

Lucy teared up. "I'm afraid you are entirely right," she whispered.

As Henry broke into a smile, she felt a million suns rise.

"Miss Catherine Edgewood. Lucibelle Bellini. Lucy Bell." His laughing eyes grew tender. "My one and only Lucy. Would you do me the honour of becoming my wife?"

"Oh yes," her voice wobbled. "Yes. Please." She laughed through her tears.

He kissed her, tenderly and slowly, as if he knew they had all the time in the world.

Lucy melted into his arms.

I'm at home, she thought. *Finally.*

LUCY AND THE DUKE OF SECRETS

An insistent yipping by their feet caused them to break apart, laughing.

"Bartimaeus. Who played a leading role in this entire affair. What would we have done without you?" Henry picked up the little pup, and together they returned to the dining room.

The dowager raised her quizzing glass when the couple entered, arm in arm.

"First she is a housemaid, then a prank-playing friend, the daughter of a pair of itinerant acting dwarves, a governess, a Drury Lane actress, a Viscount's daughter, and now, appearing from the besotted look on my grandson's face, the next Duchess of Ashmore. Pray make up your mind who you are."

"Miss Lucy Bell—also known as Miss Catherine Edgewood, has just given me the great happiness of accepting to be my duchess."

The entire company was unsurprised but delighted.

Arabella hugged Lucy. "I knew it," she whispered into her ears. "I'm so glad to have you as a sister."

The dowager sniffed. "I see you finally had the good sense to put my grandson out of his misery. It wasn't to be borne. He is beaming. Ashford never beams. Now this is accomplished, can we finally proceed to having some tea?"

EPILOGUE

1819, ASHMORE HALL, OXFORDSHIRE.

*A*rabella stared at the newspaper.

They were having tea outside, since it was a sunny, warm day. Her grandmama had just retired, and Ash carried a mewling baby in his arms, two-month-old Lady Isolde Rosamunde Kunigunde, while Bartimaeus, who'd grown considerably, trotted after him.

"What a brilliant idea. Let's go to London and watch *Lionel & Clarissa*," Lucy said. She was softer, and there was a dreamy, contented look in her eyes that her younger self had never had. "It'll be amusing, for the subtitle is 'the school for fathers,' so it's positively mandatory for Ashmore to see. Arabella, did you hear?"

"Hm?" She looked up, blinking.

"The comic opera. London."

"So?"

"You said you'd wanted to see it."

She set the paper aside. "Oh, yes. I did. Didn't I?"

"I was suggesting to Ash that we could go in a fortnight?"

Arabella shook herself. "Yes. Absolutely, let's go. Brilliant."

Lucy tilted her curly head to one side. "Are you feeling well, Arabella?"

Arabella smiled back at her friend. "Couldn't be happier."

"Good. You seem so quiet these days."

"Remember the wishing well, Lucy?"

Lucy laughed. "How could I ever forget? That blasted well started it off. What a disaster it was."

"I never asked you about that night. What did you wish for?"

Lucy grinned. "Nothing that ever came true, alas. That Miss Hilversham would let us spend some time at the seaside. It never happened. Superstitious nonsense."

Arabella looked at her oddly. "How curious of you to say so. You ended up marrying a duke."

Lucy stared at her. "Do you believe me marrying Henry had something to do with your wish?"

"Of course. Look at you. Happy end and all."

Lucy took Arabella's hands in her own. "You'll find your happy end, too."

Arabella smiled tightly. "If I could, I would, like Pen, climb back into the well and change the wish. Not that I really believe in it."

"Dukes are not so bad, after all." Lucy looked fondly at Ashmore, who was walking with the baby in the rose garden.

"Yes. But not for me," Arabella muttered to herself.

Lucy didn't hear her. "We could visit Miss Hilversham after we return from London."

"That's a fabulous idea, Lucy."

"Wonderful. I'll tell Mrs Bates of our plans." Lucy left.

Arabella looked around furtively to check whether no one was around. Then she quickly tore out a small section of the newspaper and tucked it into her bodice. She folded up the remaining newspaper and gave it to a footman, with the instructions to have it burned.

DEEP IN THE WISHING WELL OF 24 PARADISE ROW, THREE coins glittered mysteriously in the turquoise waters.

Being a duke's daughter is not all it's cracked up to be.... When Arabella runs away to become a governess, she finds herself hired by a most peculiar family ... and a dashingly handsome blacksmith. Don't miss Arabella's and Philip's story in *Arabella and the Reluctant Duke*!

ACKNOWLEDGMENTS

I could not have written this book without the help of those who have been incredibly supportive on this exhilarating creative ride.

Many thanks to Amanda Howard, amazing critique partner and writing buddy, for having slogged through early drafts with unerring patience. Thank you for all your generous feedback and wonderful support.

My dear friend Maria Ribera, my Romance Super Reader and on-site research expert, for your unfailing enthusiasm and your words of encouragement. You were the first to believe that I could do this! Thank you.

Lastly, to my husband and children, who were endlessly patient with me and who cheered me on from the sideline. I am blessed to have you in my life.

A NOTE FROM SOFI

Claim your FREE copy of *Wishing for a Duke* to find out what happened that fateful night at the wishing well:

When a midnight visit to a wishing well ends in disaster, the Duke of Ashmore, whom Lucy secretly admires, blames Lucy and withdraws his sister from the seminary. Lucy's been in trouble before, but never anything like this...

Get your copy here: www.sofilaporte.com/newsletter-1

ARABELLA AND THE RELUCTANT DUKE

EXCERPT

CHAPTER 1

*L*ady Arabella Astley, sister of the Duke of Ashmore, wished she was better at lying. In her entire twenty-two years of life, Arabella had never lied. Lately, she'd resorted to lying as if it were her second skin. It was rather exhausting. Her name, which she'd changed to plain Miss Arabella Weston, would take a while to get used to. Her new identity as a governess even more so. She was exhausted from the coach ride, dusty from the walk to the cottage, and she had a sinking feeling of certainty that coming to Cornwall to answer the advertisement for the position of a governess had been a foolhardy undertaking. To top it all, she was being interviewed by a mere girl.

"What do you mean you don't have any references?" Miss Katy Merivale's forehead puckered to a frown. Arabella stared at her in fascination. Wisps of dark hair escaped from the girl's thick, messy braids, and her blue gingham cotton dress seemed a tad too short and had patches at the elbow. How old could she be? Sixteen? Younger?

"Miss Weston?" The girl's voice tore Arabella out of her thoughts. "References?"

Arabella squirmed in the rickety kitchen chair. Of course she did not have any references. A Duke's daughter did not need any. But governesses were a different matter altogether. Arabella suppressed a groan. Why hadn't she thought of that? She searched the tiny, cramped kitchen for inspiration. What an odd place for a job interview. But as the parlour room had been uninhabitable, Miss Katy had explained, the kitchen was the only other available place. She'd led her here as if it were the most natural thing in the world. Arabella had been too stunned to even blink. It was the first time for her to have ever set foot in a kitchen. She fixated on the chipped crockery on the sooty fireplace's mantlepiece as if they could provide references. Sweat pooled in her armpits, for her maid's rough linen dress was too warm and spanned too tightly around her chest.

She licked her lips and decided that the truth was always the best. "This would be my first position as a governess."

"That's not good. We can't hire you without references." Miss Katy propped both elbows on the table and chewed her lower lip.

Arabella shifted in her chair. "But I do have my report cards here, from Miss Hilversham's Seminary of Young Ladies in Bath." She pulled out several sheaves of paper. "Sorry about the smudge. Some tea spilt on it." Conveniently right over where her real name was supposed to be, rendering it illegible. It had taken some dexterity to topple the teacup over in a manner that wouldn't drench the entire document.

Miss Katy's green eyes grew huge behind her glasses. "You had Music, Arithmetic, Science, Literature, Languages,

Deportment and Dance, Arts and Theatre, and History." A note of awe entered her voice. "And you did excellent in all subjects."

"I enjoyed studying there."

"Which was your favourite subject?"

"I've always been partial to the languages and literature," Arabella said. She spoke the languages fluently and without any hint of an accent.

"What was it like at the Seminary?"

Arabella smiled wistfully. "Wonderful." Her years at the Seminary with her friends Lucy, Birdie, and Pen had been some of the best she'd ever experienced.

"Did you sleep there?" There was a catch in Miss Katy's voice.

"Oh, yes, it was a boarding school."

"Did you share a room with someone?"

"Yes. My roommate was called Lucy." Arabella smiled involuntarily. "She is like a sister to me."

Miss Katy lowered her voice. "Did you — did you sneak out at night sometimes?"

Arabella lowered hers as well. "Oh yes. Several times. We visited graveyards, and once we went to a wishing well at midnight..." That particular adventure hadn't ended well, with herself falling into the well. Arabella shook herself. "Back to the position I am applying for. I'd very much like to have this position. Not to offend you, but shouldn't I be talking to your mother?"

The girl shook her head. "Mama is dead."

"I am so very sorry." Arabella drew her eyebrows together. "But shouldn't your father be conducting this interview, then?"

Miss Katy jumped up from her chair. "Papa doesn't have time for things like this."

"Excuse me, but how old are you?"

"I am fourteen."

"Fourteen!" Her precociousness made her appear older.

Miss Katy stuck her nose in the air. "It's just a number. I am the mistress of the house. And I say —" She hesitated, tilting her head to the side, as if weighing up the lack of references with her experience at the Seminary. "I say that you get the job. You're hired."

Arabella pursed her lips. "That's wonderful, but I would like to have a word with your father, if that is possible. To finalise a few things."

"He won't be very happy if we disturb him. As I said, he's very busy." Miss Katy proceeded to fill a kettle with water and set it on the stove to boil. "Would you like some tea?"

Tea would be divine. Tea, and a bath. And a long nap in her very own four-poster bed...

"Yes, please. I mean, no, thank you. About your father. Surely, five minutes of his time is not too much to ask?" Arabella got up, picked up her papers and paused.

The girl fidgeted and pulled on her braids.

A sharp clanking came from the back of the house, making Arabella jump. It sounded like the hitting of a hammer on iron. Before she could ask what that was, the door crashed open and the kitchen was filled with havoc and mayhem.

A little girl came shrieking into the kitchen, followed by a boy with tousled hair, who was shrieking with equal force. They ran around the table two, three times, before Katy caught the little one.

"Joy! Robin! Quieeeeet!" she shouted.

There was a momentary silence.

"I say, Katy, I just needed to try out my newest experiment on Joy, but she won't let me!" Robin said after he'd caught his breath.

"No!" Joy screamed with all the full force her lungs could muster.

"Yes!" Robin shouted back.

"Quiet!" Katy shouted over both of them.

"But she won't let me try out the experiment!" Robin threw up his hands.

"Because I don't want to!" Joy crossed her arms and stomped her foot. She wore an odd contraption on her head with several antlers.

"What on earth are you trying to accomplish, Robin Merivale?" Katy asked, sternly.

"It's my newest invention. An invisibility machine! All I have to do is attach that wire there to this wire here, and she'll be invisible!"

"Nooo!" Joy wailed.

"Fine," Robin said, clearly frustrated. "Then give me the machine back. I'll try it on Whitepaw."

"No! Don't you dare hurt Whitepaw!"

"Don't be a goose, no one's going to hurt that cat. Try it yourself and you will see!"

"No!" Joy wailed as if the world was about to end.

"Will you just stop shouting, both of you? We have a visitor here."

Both children froze and turned, wide-eyed, towards Arabella, who clutched her reticule and bonnet. She stared back at them, horrified.

"This is Robin, he is ten. And the little one is Joy, she is four. This is Miss Weston. She is going to be our new governess," Katy explained.

Both children's eyes grew round. Joy's mouth dropped.

"Now, that hasn't been finalised — " Arabella took a slight step back.

"It's as good as decided." Katy set her mouth stubbornly.

Arabella sighed.

Master Robin looked at her, scepticism written all over his face. "Can you teach me about the mechanics of engineering?"

"Engineering? Well...." How to answer that question? It looked like her second round of interviewing had begun, and it might be more demanding than the first.

"Do you know anything about steam engines?" he demanded.

"I have read about them in the paper."

"Aeronautics machines?"

"You mean hydrogen balloons?" Arabella's face brightened. She'd attended a balloon launch with her brother, the Duke of Ashmore, several years ago. "I've actually been in one."

Master Robin's jaw nearly dropped to the ground. "Nooo. You've been on a manned hydrogen balloon flight?"

"I just went up and down, but it was the most exhilarating experience in my entire life."

"You actually were *in* a balloon as it went up?"

Arabella nodded. No need to tell Robin the balloon had risen only a few feet before her brother had insisted to let her down again. He himself hadn't gone along because he was afraid of heights.

"Capital! What was it like? Were the people really small and the houses and trees and did you have the feeling of weightlessness, of f–f–flying?" he stuttered in his excitement.

"Well, yes."

"Did you know the first man who flew across the channel —"

"Jean–Pierre Blanchard." That much she knew. She'd read an article on him in the Times.

Robin's eyes glistened with hero–worship. "It took him only two and a half hours to fly from Dover to France. In a gas balloon. Lighter than air!"

A little hand slipped into hers. Joy looked up at her. She'd taken off the metal contraption. "I'm Joy." She grinned shyly at Arabella. She had a head of unruly blonde curls and dimples in her chubby cheeks.

Arabella melted. "I'm happy to meet you, Miss Joy."

"I can read," the girl told her.

"How very clever of you. What is your favourite book?"

She titled her head sideways and considered Arabella. "Mouse."

"That sounds like a lovely book."

"*The Life and Perambulations of a Mouse* by Dorothy Kilner. Papa reads it to her every night." Katy rolled her eyes. "It's a dreadfully dull book, so Papa has to invent most of the story."

Arabella looked around. Three solemn pairs of eyes looked at her expectantly.

"Does Papa know you've hired a governess? I thought he didn't want one." Robin turned to Katy.

Katy pulled invisible threads from the sleeve of her faded blue gingham dress.

Arabella knit her brows. "What do you mean, he didn't want one?"

"Katy, don't tell me you didn't tell Papa?" Robin rolled his eyes. "She does this all the time you know. She likes to do things without Papa's permission."

"Wait." A pang of alarm went through Arabella. "Are you saying you hired me without your father's knowledge?"

"Um." Katy avoided Arabella's eyes.

"Are you saying your father did not send the job advertisement to the Times?" Arabella pressed further.

"Papa doesn't want to hire a governess. Doesn't see the need," Robin explained. "But if you know all about hydrogen balloons then that's capital, and I don't mind." His eyes brightened again.

"We need a governess. Just look at us. What can I do if

Papa doesn't think of things like that?" Katy muttered and waved her arm about vaguely.

"But, Miss Katy, this is just not how things are done. If your father hasn't consented to this, how could I possibly take the position?" She shook her head.

Outside the clanking continued.

"Why don't you just ask him? He's out back." Robin sat down at the table and started to fiddle around with the wires of his invisibility machine.

Katy gave up, defeated. "Very well. He's bound to find out sooner or later, anyhow."

Arabella put on her bonnet and went outside. She followed the clanking noise that came from the back of the house. She heard a baritone voice utter a curse. Then she froze and took a sharp intake of breath. For in front of her stood a man, hammering wildly on an anvil. His thick auburn hair stuck out madly in all directions. Heat emanated from his body. And he was naked.

ALSO BY SOFI LAPORTE

ABOUT THE AUTHOR

Sofi was born in Vienna, grew up in Seoul, studied Comparative Literature in Maryland, U.S.A., and lived in Quito with her Ecuadorian husband. When not writing, she likes to scramble about the countryside exploring medieval castle ruins. She currently lives with her husband, 3 trilingual children, a sassy cat and a cheeky dog in Europe.

Get in touch and visit Sofi at her Website, on Facebook or Instagram!

amazon.com/Sofi-Laporte/e/B07N1K8H6C
facebook.com/sofilaporteauthor
instagram.com/sofilaporteauthor
bookbub.com/profile/sofi-laporte

Printed in Great Britain
by Amazon

44473483R10128